"You're freezing up on me, aren't you?" he said.

Gillian tried to sound calm and unflustered. "I don't usually make love in the back seat of a car."

"No? Where *do* you usually make love, then?" His eyes sparkled mischievously.

"That's my business," she said firmly.

"I don't think so. I think it's mine. That's twice you've let me melt you up to a point. Then you've made a mad dash back to the freezer. What gives? I know you want me"—his voice became husky—"and God knows I want you."

Dear Reader:

As the months go by, we continue to receive word from you that SECOND CHANCE AT LOVE romances are providing you with the kind of romantic entertainment you're looking for. In your letters you've voiced enthusiastic support for SECOND CHANCE AT LOVE, you've shared your thoughts on how personally meaningful the books are, and you've suggested ideas and changes for future books. Although we can't always reply to your letters as quickly as we'd like, please be assured that we appreciate your comments. Your thoughts are all-important to us!

We're glad many of you have come to associate SECOND CHANCE AT LOVE books with our butterfly trademark. We think the butterfly is a perfect symbol of the reaffirmation of life and thrilling new love that SECOND CHANCE AT LOVE heroines and heroes find together in each story. We hope you keep asking for the "butterfly books," and that, when you buy one—whether by a favorite author or a talented new writer—you're sure of a good read. You can trust all SECOND CHANCE AT LOVE books to live up to the high standards of romantic fiction you've come to expect.

So happy reading, and keep your letters coming!

With warm wishes,

Ellen Edwards

Ellen Edwards
SECOND CHANCE AT LOVE
The Berkley/Jove Publishing Group
200 Madison Avenue
New York, NY 10016

Second Chance at Love

FORBIDDEN RAPTURE
KATE NEVINS

A
SECOND CHANCE AT LOVE
BOOK

FORBIDDEN RAPTURE

chapter 1

"I GUESS YOU'VE been here before, Miss West."

She glanced around Peking's modern, efficient airport. "Yes, just about a year ago, Dan. My name's Gillian, by the way."

"Sure thing, Gillian."

A grin flashed white across his regular bronzed features. He tossed a longish blond strand out of his eyes.

"Are you from California?" she asked with a smile.

"Malibu. It shows even without the surfboard, huh? I'm starting to lose my tan, though."

This husky surfer with bleached hair whom Griffon Films had sent to meet her was at least her age, Gillian thought. But he seemed boyish, and younger than twenty-eight.

"I bet you're tired, Gillian. It's a long trip from Boston."

"Actually, I'm not. Your studio got me a first-class sleeperette on the plane to Japan, and then I spent the night in Tokyo before coming on to Beijing, or Peking, whichever you want to call it. By the way, thanks for coming to the airport."

"No sweat; it's my job. I'm Burke Ferrara's production assistant, his gofer. Only, I don't usually get to go for a good-looking girl like you."

He grinned at his own joke, but Gillian only smiled politely. Her heart had skipped a beat at his casual mention of Burke Ferrara. It had suddenly made real the fact that she was actually here in Peking and on the verge of meeting the famous director. She was a little nervous too. Even a professor of Chinese at a prestigious New England college still had within her the young girl who had absorbed the glamour of Hollywood along with her box of popcorn.

"I've got a car with a driver outside," Dan was saying now. "Do you want to go to the hotel or the set first?"

"The set, please. I'm dying to get started."

The car was a four-door made-in-China sedan called the Shanghai, which came in three colors—gray, navy, and black. This one was gray, and the driver was wearing a gray tunic and baggy pants to match the paint job.

Gillian greeted him with the customary *nee how mah,* or "Hi, how are you?" and followed it up with a few questions about the weather in Peking. The driver flashed the bright smile all Chinese did when a "round-eye" spoke their language, and answered her with a stream of Chinese, which included his name, Keng.

"Hey, you speak Chinese pretty well. Where'd you learn it?" Dan asked.

"My grandfather managed an American bank in Shanghai in the Thirties and took the trouble to learn Chinese. He used to tell me stories about China when I was a little girl, and taught me a few Chinese words and phrases. When I went to college, it seemed natural to major in Chinese. Then after grad school I got a job teaching it."

"So how'd you feel when Griffon Films tapped you for this job?"

Gillian laughed her throaty laugh. "Excited, thrilled, happy. Okay?"

"All *right!*"

"Seriously, though, it sounded like fun to be the historical consultant for a movie. It's my area of expertise — the Boxer Rebellion — so I was sure I could handle it. And it gave me the chance to come back to China."

"How'd you get the time off from teaching?"

"Oh, it was a plus for the college to have one of their faculty chosen as consultant for a big movie. I certainly give Mr. Ferrara a lot of credit for wanting his film to be historically accurate."

Dan bent his head to hide a grin. "It wasn't *Burke* who wanted a consultant. It was the studio. They insisted."

Gillian turned away toward the window, distressed by what she had just heard. Griffon Studios had forced her on Burke Ferrara. The job she had so looked forward to was caving in before she even got started.

Subliminally she noticed that they were on a side road now. The fields of green rapeseed and beans had given way to spears of golden wheat. Then a bamboo fence came in view.

"This is it," Dan said. "We put the fence up to keep onlookers away, but it's practically impossible to keep them all out. We've had crowd scenes you wouldn't believe."

In spite of her disappointment Gillian was curious and excited, intensely eager to see how the movie company would act out the story of *Siege*.

She walked through a gate in the fence, guarded by a Chinese with a badge, and onto a dusty, unpaved street lined with crowded shops and outdoor markets. It was the Peking of 1900 superimposed on a Chinese village of today.

Pigtailed Chinese walked along the street, balancing poles, with bundles attached across their shoulders. Coolies in ragged clothes tottered by, bent double under loads too heavy for them. Other coolies, half-naked, pulled rickshaws like human horses, their passengers either finely dressed Chinese or beefy, red-faced Westerners.

A sedan chair passed, curtains closed. They opened suddenly, and a woman—American or European—looked out. She raised her gloved hand to two other women in plumed hats, long skirts, and fitted jackets, walking among the crowd of Chinese.

That's wrong, Gillian breathed. Definitely wrong. She glanced toward the array of cameras shooting the scene. And at the man sprawled in a chair, watching.

He sat, broad shoulders hunched forward, hands in the pockets of brown corduroy pants, his long, powerful-looking legs stretched out before him. A blue denim jacket was buttoned up against the dust a machine was swirling around the set. A brown corduroy cap half-covered straight dark hair that fell to the nape of his neck.

There was tremendous tension in his bearing and in the set of his bold profile. Yet Gillian didn't have the impression of nervousness. His was a dynamic energy, like that of a coiled steel spring waiting to be released when needed.

As if sensing he was being looked at, he turned. His eyes were an exquisite blue. There was no other color in them—no washed-out gray, no cat's-eye yellow, no flecks of brown. And they were fringed with heavy dark lashes.

A lean brown hawklike face emphasized those soft midnight-blue eyes even more. Velvet and steel. That's what Burke Ferrara made her think of.

A shift in relationships occurred. She was no longer the observer, but the observed. For a long minute, his penetrating gaze roved willfully over her, lingering on the high rounded breasts, the small waist, the long, slender legs.

She wasn't used to being looked at like that. The men

she met at academic conferences didn't. She crisped her lips and turned her head sharply. But his gaze had awakened something strange in Gillian—an excitement, almost a feeling of sensual intimacy with this man who, according to Dan, was already her undeclared opponent.

Then Ferrara was yelling, "Terrific! It's a wrap," and the scene dissolved before her. The Western ladies lifted their skirts above their knees and dashed for the dressing-room trailers. The merchants drifted off the set, chattering in Chinese. The sweating coolies wiped off the water that had been splashed on their bare torsos and ran for a pile of quilted jackets on the ground.

Gillian followed with awestruck eyes the tall, dark-haired actress who had been one of the pair of women walking on the street.

"Is that Andrea Steele?" she asked Dan. "The one going into the trailer now?"

"Yes. She has her own dressing room, because she's the star. Listen, I want to introduce you to Burke." Dan started a grin that kept going till Gillian asked, "What's the joke?"

"Nothing. I just can't wait till Burke meets you."

"Something wrong?" Gillian asked a little frostily, looking down at her plum-colored wool pants suit and fuchsia silk shirt.

"Not with you!" Dan said emphatically. "It's just that Burke expected somebody a little different. You know, more like a historical consultant."

"I could have come dressed as a book, I suppose."

Her sarcasm was lost on Dan, who had grabbed her elbow with a "C'mon" and started to propel her toward Ferrara.

"*You're* my historical consultant?" Ferrara said after Dan had introduced them. "I thought you were somebody's friend visiting the set."

Gillian laughed. "A slight correction, Mr. Ferrara. Not *your* historical consultant. The *studio's*."

There was a quick knitting together of his brows so

they formed a single dark line across his tanned forehead. At the same time his hand tightened on hers. What had started as a formal handshake was turning into a challenge. The pressure of his hand wasn't painful; if anything, it was too pleasurable. She could feel the warmth of his skin, his sinewy fingers, the push of his thumb against her palm. The strength and sensuousness of his touch disturbed her, and she started to breathe a little fast. She tried to withdraw her hand, but he held onto it all the time he studied her with an openness that had nothing to do with good manners.

She knew what he saw—an oval, small-boned face, the nose powdered with faint freckles, straight taffy-brown hair, thick and lustrous, falling like heavy rain from a center part, and brown eyes too big for her face, or any face, she thought. When she was a little girl, she had gone around squinting to make them look smaller. When she was older, boys started telling her what beautiful eyes she had. She still hadn't believed it, but she had stopped squinting.

Ferrara finally dropped her hand and suddenly became all business. "I want to talk to you, Miss West." His eyes swept over the set. "Unfortunately I don't know where. We're short of trailers, and I gave mine up to alleviate some of the overcrowding. I can see the office and props trailers are being used just now. Ah, there's an empty one."

Hands in his pockets, he set off with a long, loose-jointed stride. Gillian raised her eyebrows and followed. She started rehearsing mentally what she would tell him had been wrong with the scene just played but found her attention quickly diverted to Burke Ferrara himself. The confident sweep of the broad shoulders ahead of her, the lean hips under the corduroy jeans, the utter maleness of his form became the focal point of her thoughts.

She remembered reading somewhere that he was forty, that he had once been married to Andrea Steele. Gillian couldn't recall any other wives, but there had been plenty of women.

"Burke Ferrara at the premiere of his latest smash hit with the well-known star . . ." was a familiar photo caption.

With an effort she forced her thoughts away from the director and focused them on *Siege* so she'd be prepared to defend her criticism of the sedan chair scene.

The film was a love story set against the background of the Boxer Rebellion, the uprising in 1900 of a fanatic patriotic organization against the foreign colonialists on Chinese soil. It climaxed in a sixty-day siege by the Boxers of the Western powers, and Japan's diplomatic legations in Peking. An international force finally lifted the siege, and the subsequent sack of Peking by troops and civilians was brutal and thorough.

Siege tells the story of a high-spirited woman who, under the stress of siege conditions, sees her husband, an American consular official, for the first time as he really is—cowardly, petty, and selfish. The daily danger and hardships of siege life also make her reckless. She seeks the love she needs in the arms of a lieutenant in the small detachment of U. S. Marines guarding the legations.

They make plans to go away together if they survive, but when the siege is over she decides to stay with her husband, because a divorce or any hint of scandal would hurt his career. And the lieutenant marries the young girl who has been a guest at the legation during the siege.

The lovers come together again in France during the First World War. Her husband has been assigned to Paris. She volunteers to drive a Red Cross ambulance at the front and meets the lieutenant, now a captain.

They spend the night together in a village inn near the front lines. When they leave in the morning, they encounter a captured German officer who has often been a guest at her dinner table in Peking. They stop and talk about old times. During the conversation the German lets it slip that the woman's husband had been his wife's lover during the siege.

The officer is marched off in a group of prisoners by a squad of marines. The woman, realizing her sacrifice has been for nothing, drives her ambulance down a road toward an area she's been warned about, a section that's being shelled.

Gillian knew Griffon Films hoped to distribute the film in China and therefore wanted it to be historically accurate. And as a scholar of Chinese history, truth was important to her. More than important, it was the very foundation of her profession as she saw it. Apparently, it was less important to Burke Ferrara.

She caught up with him now as he returned the waves of three girls who had just left the trailer he was headed for.

"That takes them back to the hotel," he explained, pointing to the bus toward which the girls were walking. "You'll be using that too. We all do, to get to where we're shooting, which is pretty much all over the city. But a couple of cars and drivers have been put at our disposal too, so don't hesitate to ask for one if you need it."

The trailer smelled as though it had been doused in perfume. Jars of cosmetics littered two makeshift tables with mirrors. Long skirts and ruffled shirtwaists were draped over chairs or hung up untidily on a rope strung across one end.

"Damn, what a mess!" Burke exclaimed. "I'll have to tell Dan to get after those girls. Here, sit here." He tossed a couple of skirts off a chair, and Gillian sat down. Clearing the only other chair in the trailer, he placed it facing Gillian and threw himself into it. Legs stretched out in front of him, hands in his pockets, he regarded her steadily.

"Even with the door open, we're not going to be able to breathe this air for more than five minutes, so I'll just tell you what I expect from you, and you can ask questions later. Okay?"

Gillian's soft brown eyes darkened with displeasure. She wasn't used to being treated this way. The people who frequented the halls of academe were much less blunt. But she nodded slightly to show she understood.

"To be quite frank, I don't want you here—the studio does. It's nothing personal—I'm just afraid you'll slow us down. And it'll all be unnecessary. The studio hopes to show this movie in China as well as at home, but it's not a documentary. The Chinese know what happened during the Boxer Rebellion. They don't need an educational film about it. And the American audience will be primarily interested in the story. The *story*'s the reason—the only reason—for the film. The background needs to be accurate only in a general sort of way."

Gillian flared up. How could anything be accurate in a "general sort of way"?

"You can't create a historically accurate background without paying attention to detail," she said hotly. "For example, in the scene you just shot..."

"Yes?" There was something dangerous in the way he said it and in the narrowing of his sea-blue eyes, but Gillian plunged ahead.

"Western women didn't walk in Chinese cities in those days. There were lots of reasons. They might be jostled, the smells were bad, and they didn't have to—there were rickshaws and sedan chairs."

Ferrara sat up and took his hands out of his pockets. He smiled sarcastically.

"Did you also happen to notice that my ladies were jostled by a coolie who unexpectedly did not step aside for them, that they registered surprise when he didn't, and that the surprise turned to horrified shock when they read the sign on the building opposite: 'Foreign Devils Get Out'?"

"Written in English, of course."

"I think the American audience would find Chinese

characters a little difficult to read, don't you, Miss West? Presumably the Boxers made the signs to be read by the English and Americans in their country. The point I want to make with that scene is that the Boxer uprising is coming. Coolies no longer step aside for Western ladies. I could hardly make that point if the ladies were riding in a sedan chair, could I? And the audience couldn't see their expression if they were peeking at that sign from behind closed curtains.

"Or maybe in your infinite knowledge of film making, you think I should have them peek out, see the sign, shriek, and throw up their hands in a dead faint."

Her eyes were incandescent with anger now, but she kept her voice cool. "I suppose a highly versatile director could find a way to convey the information that things were changing in old Peking on the eve of the uprising at the same time that he was historically accurate."

"Highly versatile or not," Ferrara said, his words measured like bullets, "this director says what goes into his scenes and what doesn't. And those women are walking the streets."

"And if you get to show your movie here, that's exactly what they'll look like to the Chinese—streetwalkers!"

"Let's go back to square one," he was saying now with exaggerated patience. "Your job is to ride herd on historical detail for the studio. Right?"

Gillian didn't give him the satisfaction of an answer.

"Maybe if they question something we do, if you could persuade them of the rightness of our approach, you might be useful."

"Whether I think it's right or not?" she said contemptuously.

"Miss Puritan Conscience," he said wearily, "I've got a picture to make. We're behind schedule already and we're sure to go over budget. The Chinese are very cooperative, but East is East and West is West, and I'm not sure they should be making movies together. Their technicians work differently, there's the language barrier even with interpreters, their conception of time is different from ours, equipment has had to be improvised, and now you have to come along with this historical crap. Hell, I've been here a month and I haven't even seen the Great Wall yet. So gimme a break, will ya? Just do as I say, collect your nice packet of money, enjoy your trip to Peking, then go home and teach Chinese to those preppy students in your little New England college."

She was on her feet, facing him. Her eyes snapped with anger, her breast heaved. Subliminally she took in the look of admiration that crossed his face. The raw sensuousness of it increased her fury. Instead of being treated as an equal opponent, she had been turned into an object of visual rape.

"I was hired by Griffon Studios, not by you, Mr. Ferrara. And I'll call the shots as *I* see them, not as you tell me to." She spat out the words, coating them with all the contempt she felt for him. Then she strode out of the trailer, banging the door closed behind her.

Outside she took huge gulps of the fresh, cool air. Her head ached from the heavy perfume in the trailer and from her impotent rage. And it was impotent, she had to admit as she walked across the set and gradually calmed down. Whose orders would she obey but Ferrara's? How could she expect a film studio thousands of miles away to take her side, a young associate professor of Chinese, against one of their hot-shot directors? Then what was the alternative? To go back home?

Gillian stared down at the gray pebbly dirt as she walked. She had never given up. She didn't believe in it. No West ever had. Or so the family myths went.

She looked up and saw Keng lounging against the Shanghai, a cigarette in his mouth. He had the only available car. And out of the dozens of identical bikes she had noticed when she arrived, there was only one left, drawn up to the wall under a chalked sign, "Company Bike."

Everybody had gone. Ferrara too, probably—she had heard a car start. If he had left Keng for her, it must have been because he had another car and driver.

A long bike ride through the countryside was just what she needed after the sedentary plane trip. Besides, there was nothing like exercise for working off frustration, and she was simmering with it. She had never met a man she disliked as much as she did Burke Ferrara. He was arrogant, macho, patronizing, unreasonable, unfair, manipulative, *and* domineering. Her thoughts veered between the joy of taking the first wide-bodied jet back to Boston and the pleasure it would give her to stay and be a thorn in his side.

There was no one to ask about the bike, so she told Keng she was going to ride it to the White Cloud Hotel and asked him to please take her bags there. The White Cloud, Dan had told her, was where everyone—cast, crew, and stars alike—was staying because the democratic Burke Ferrara had insisted on the same hotel for all.

"Sure, he's democratic," she muttered out loud as she wheeled the bicycle away from the wall. "Democratic like Genghis Khan. Everybody's equally under his thumb, doing what he tells them to."

Then she noticed that the name painted on the bike in Chinese characters was Flying Pigeon, and she laughed.

"Come on, Pigeon, let's fly," she said gaily, and pushed off.

She wasn't afraid of getting lost. She could read the road signs and ask for directions. Besides, she had a pretty good idea herself of which way to go.

Poplars filled the spaces unevenly along the road. It was late March, and they hadn't started to bud yet. Beyond the trees were the low gray buildings and tiled roofs of communal farms. And the bicycles that lined the road were hung with string bags holding green cabbages or an occasional protesting duck imprisoned in a wire-mesh cage. The bells rang like wind chimes. The riders stared resolutely ahead. The legs in baggy blue pants—worn by men and women alike—went like pistons, steadily forging the bikes onward.

The air was cool enough to make bicycling comfortable. But the gray sky, gray buildings, and steel-gray water of a nearby canal didn't invite strong emotions. And the rhythmic exercise combined with the pastoral surroundings lulled Gillian into a serene state where anger was impossible. To keep it that way, every time Burke Ferrara came into her mind, she pedaled faster.

Still, she couldn't keep her thoughts off him altogether. She was particularly fascinated by the idea of the director's working on a film with his ex-wife. Hollywood certainly was different from Haywood College. One of the reasons she had been so glad to come to China was that Elliot was still at Haywood. Although she was as sophisticated as the next woman, it still was a bit much, seeing your "ex" constantly at faculty teas, drama-department performances of experimental plays, and in the college library, when your divorce papers were still warm in your hands.

Riding along, she also replayed in her mind certain Ferrara movies she had seen, movies she had made a particular point to see after reading the reviews. Ferrara was known for his character studies. He was interested in how people behaved under stress. But according to the reviews, his films didn't just coldly probe the psychology of his characters; they were compassionate, emotional explorations of the human condition. And somehow he had managed to please both the critics and the general public, because his films did well at the box office too.

As she approached Peking, Gillian started riding five abreast with other bicyclists, who invariably did a double take when they saw her, then grinned broadly and sometimes waved. There were more trucks and buses on the road now too. The noise was no off-again, on-again affair, but a steady, continuous honking of horns and peal of bicycle bells.

Then the gray brick buildings of the White Cloud Hotel came in sight. The White Cloud was one of the older hotels in Peking, set in a parklike area on the outskirts and built in the traditional style of upswept eaves and green tiled roofs.

Gillian dismounted at Building Number Three, where Dan had said the film company's rooms were, and mentally marked the place where she put Flying Pigeon so it could be picked up later.

Running up the broad stone steps Gillian contemplated once more whether she should stay and try to get along with Burke Ferrara or bail out while she still could. As she entered the marble lobby the desk clerk smiled a greeting through his office window. But Gillian hadn't noticed. Her attention was riveted on the scene being played out before her in the center of the high-ceilinged columned hall.

chapter 2

A THIRTYISH-LOOKING BLONDE whose long wavy hair joined the writhings of the green dragon on the back of her red silk robe was stamping a slippered foot on the tile floor and screaming at Burke Ferrara.

"They've got to move me. I won't stay in that room another night. It's already rented—to a family of mice. *You're* the director. *You're* in charge. Tell One Fang that." The words came out slurred, but the tone was loud and commanding.

A muscle in Burke's right cheek twitched visibly. "Watch your language, Robyn," he said in a low, firm voice. "We're guests in this country. And you can't be moved. Dan's already told you that. There isn't another room vacant. Also, you've been told again and again there aren't any mice in your room."

The blonde's voice dropped an octave and iced up. "Are you suggesting I'm seeing things?"

"It's the d.t.'s," Dan said scornfully, under his breath but still audibly.

Robyn whirled around. "I heard that, Ross. And for your information, you don't get the d.t.'s from an occasional Scotch."

"Occasional!"

"Hang ten, surfer boy. Better yet, hang twenty, you gorilla."

"All right, knock it off, you two. We'll try again, Robyn." Gillian didn't think he had seen her, but Burke half-turned and said, "Miss West, would you mind explaining in Chinese to the boy at the desk that there may be mice in one of our rooms. Sometimes they understand less English than we think."

"Tell him there's a hole in the wall," Robyn called out, "and they go in and out of there like hookers in a Forty-second Street motel. Tell him all he has to do is plug it up."

"I'll do that," Gillian answered.

The window was three-deep in hotel personnel, obviously enjoying this free sample of Western-style acting. Politely the boy on duty expressed doubt that there had been a mouse in one of the hotel's rooms, but if there was a hole, he would certainly see that it was filled.

Gillian turned around to give Robyn this information and was surprised to see that Burke had left.

"Thanks," the actress said when Gillian finished. "We haven't met. I'm Robyn St. Regis. Be a pal and come upstairs with me till they fix the hole. I don't want to be in that room by myself. I'm scared stiff of mice."

"For Pete's sake, Robyn, Gillian just arrived. Why don't you let her get some rest?"

"Butt out, beach boy. When I want your advice, I'll ask for it."

"I'll go to the room with you," Gillian said in a placating tone. "But only for a few minutes. Dan's right. I would like to rest."

She told Dan where she had left the bike, then caught up with Robyn at the elevator.

"Surf bums!" Robyn muttered in a surly tone to the wall of the elevator. "They're all over the world—Miami, Oahu, St. Tropez. No brains. All they've got is sea water between the ears."

The slow-moving elevator lumbered to a stop at the second floor. Robyn started down the long corridor, and Gillian followed, wishing she was on her way to her own room instead.

She nodded to the boy seated at a desk in the hall. Like many other Chinese hotels, the doors in the White Cloud had no locks, but a kind of service station was set up on every floor for laundry collection, the delivery of extralarge thermoses of boiled water—one hot and one cold—to each room, and whatever else the guests might need. The young boys and girls assigned to these jobs all had learned a smattering of English in school.

"The star's got that room," Robyn said, pointing. "Big star—big suite." The sarcasm she aimed for was blunted by the fact that she was slurring her words badly now. She was also having trouble negotiating the worn places in the carpeting.

"You mean Andrea Steele?"

"*Queen* Andrea," Robyn corrected.

She ushered Gillian into a room with varnished wood floors and heavy old furniture. Then she flung herself across the bed, where her green dragon fought with the blue peacocks on the gaudy satin spread.

Gillian was in a hurry to leave and go to her own room. She opened the wardrobe doors briskly, looked in all the corners, and stamped her feet on the floor.

"Oh, my head," Robyn groaned. "What are you doing?"

"Letting the mice, if there are any, know you're home. They don't usually come out when there are people around. They're more afraid of you than you are of them."

"Not these Chinese mice. They love company."

Gillian looked at her speculatively. She seemed too rational for the d.t.'s, but she certainly wasn't cold sober, either.

"Where's this hole you were talking about?"

Robyn pointed a sepulchral finger toward the wardrobe. Gillian bent down and saw it then, a small hole in the molding, half-hidden by the big armoire. She was glad; better real mice than hallucinations.

"I'll call down to the desk and tell them to send a man up right away."

"Thanks. What's your name again?"

"Gillian. Gillian West."

"Thanks, Gillian."

Her voice seemed to come from the depths of a distant cavern. Gillian guessed she was falling asleep. But as Gillian was talking to the desk clerk, Robyn's voice rang out, loud and brassy as a dance hall hostess's.

"Gillian? You want a Scotch?"

"No, I'm leaving now, Robyn. I've got things to do. A hotel technician will be up soon to plug that hole, and you won't have any more problems."

"Problems! You don't know what problems are till you work for Burke Ferrara." Her voice was thick again, and her *l*'s sounded like *r*'s, as though she were Japanese.

Maybe it was unfair to interrogate the woman while she was intoxicated, but Gillian wanted to know more about Burke. Whether she stayed or left depended on what she could find out about him.

"I wouldn't know," she said lightly. "What's he like?"

"Heartless. Mean. If you can believe it, I have to share a dressing trailer. *Me! Robyn St. Regis!*"

"But I understand there's a shortage of trailers."

"Andrea Steele has one, doesn't she?"

Gillian refrained from saying that the director himself didn't.

"She thinks she's so hot. Just because she can wrap

Ferrara around her little finger. That's one babe who makes sure she comes out on top, no matter what it takes, believe me." With a sudden change of mood, Robyn started snuffling into the satin bedspread. "It's just miserable here. There's nothing to do. No shows, no night life. I miss California. I miss Hollywood."

Gillian slid Robyn's shapely limbs under the covers and put a box of tissues within easy reach.

"Go to sleep, Robyn. I'll wait for the technician."

The actress slipped off immediately into a drunken doze. A few minutes later, Gillian opened the door to a man in the usual tunic and baggy pants, who quickly filled the hole in the molding. Then, leaving the lights on, she tiptoed out and went to her own room.

It was the twin of Robyn's—the same narrow beds, huge wardrobe, and lamp with a pink silk shade on a veneered mahogany nightstand. There were also the obligatory two thermoses along with a pair of flowered porcelain cups with lids and a canister of green tea.

But she had another room as well, a sitting room furnished with a desk and a pair of armchairs with lace antimacassars. Nothing was shiny-new, but it was all clean and adequate. Besides, there were nice little touches on the desk—a calendar with the dates in Chinese, fine rice-paper stationery, pens, an inkwell filled with a thick black fluid like Texas oil, and a glue bottle for sticking stamps on postcards. Noticing her luggage for the first time, she speculated about whether she should unpack.

Gillian went to the window and looked out at the yellow globes of light in the courtyard. This wasn't China; it was Hollywood. She was in an arena with a bunch of snapping, scrapping gladiators—an imperious director, a juvenile production assistant, and a drunken, unhappy actress.

She glanced behind her at her bags. She could leave. She didn't have a contract with Griffon Studios. She could pay her own airfare and go home. People made mistakes. The thing was to get out early. She had learned that from her marriage—two years had been too long.

But she wasn't leaving. She knew that deep inside herself. And the reason was Burke Ferrara. If she had to fight him every inch of the way, she'd make *Siege* as historically accurate as she could. She owed it to her own academic tradition and to the audience that would see the film.

Just thinking about his arrogance, his condescension, and his attempt to subvert her performance of her job enraged her again. She opened her suitcase with a loud snap and started putting her clothes in the wardrobe. She was staying whether Burke Ferrara wanted her to or not.

The phone rang harshly several times. When she picked it up, she recognized Burke's sardonic growl.

"I wanted to thank you for taking care of that little matter with St. Regis."

"Not at all. I thought it was nice of you to hang around to see how it all turned out."

"Robyn has had spiders, roaches, mice, and bats in her room. No one else has."

"Does she really have the—?"

"D.t.'s?" Burke interrupted. "No, what she's doing is making star tracks."

"Star tracks?"

"Yeah. She's not a star, but she thinks if she makes tracks like one, people will think she is. I didn't mean to leave you holding the bag; I just didn't want to spend the rest of my life planting rice in China on a murder rap."

"There *was* a hole in her wall," Gillian said reproachfully. "I saw it and got the hotel to send a man up to fix it."

"If there was a hole in the wall," Burke said wearily, "I'll guarantee Robyn put it there. Listen, why don't I tell you my troubles over a drink? My conversation's not much, but I'm an interesting complainer."

"I already turned down the same offer from Robyn."

"Miss West, if you can't tell the difference between me and Robyn St. Regis, you've been shut up in that ivory tower too long."

She hesitated. Her fingers gripped the old-fashioned black telephone. Why was every encounter with this man a challenge, a gauntlet thrown down to her? His hostility was obvious. But couldn't he confine it to the set? Was she going to have to fight him after work too?

Gillian mentally prepared a refusal; she was in no mood, on her first day in China, for an evening of warfare. Then she relaxed her hold on the phone. She had changed her mind. The first rule of combat was, "Know your enemy." So be it.

"I can be ready in about forty-five minutes," she said.

"Great. You've got it. The offer includes dinner, by the way."

"Thank you, but—"

"No dining, no wining," he interrupted in a firm voice.

"Oh, in that case . . ." Her voice trailed off into an unwilling laugh.

"Forty-five minutes," he repeated forcefully. "I'll knock at your door."

Gillian showered quickly. The water that swirled around her ankles picked up rust from the gouged-out tub. If she fell, would she need a tetanus shot? she wondered, amused.

She chose a two-piece, winter-white knit dress, cut low and closed at the top by three pearl buttons. She had planned to wear it with a scarf while she was in China, out of deference to Chinese mores. She draped the pink-and-mauve scarf around her neck now and looked at herself in the mirror. The effect was pretty and very sedate. Elliot would have loved it.

With a quick movement she undid the silk triangle and tossed it on the bed. A little revealing, perhaps—the soft throat ending in a well-defined cleavage, the full, high breasts outlined by the knit—but she wasn't going to play up to Burke Ferrara's image of her as a fusty academic type.

She brushed her hair till it crackled in the dry Peking air, and let it fall over her shoulders again instead of forming it into the usual chignon. A little eye makeup and lip gloss, and she was ready. Since there were few restaurants open to foreigners in China, she had no doubt they'd be dining downstairs.

When she opened the door to Burke, he looked her up and down in a way that didn't at all suggest he was undressing her.

"Not the right clothes? We're going formal, perhaps?"

He shook his head. "We're going outside—to the International Hotel. Go get a coat."

His command nettled her. She'd freeze before she obeyed it.

"New England," she said, flexing her arm muscles. "I won't need a coat."

He shrugged, his eyes narrowing a bit. "Have it your way."

Once they were in the freight-size, freight-slow elevator, she wished she had worn the scarf. The sensual look in those dark blue sardonic eyes as they roamed over the soft globes of her breasts, her rounded hips, and slender silky legs was once more doing strange things to her.

This time the feeling of excitement that mounted in her was coupled with a wave of delicious voluptuous warmth. Without wanting to, she responded to him. Her soft brown eyes became brighter, her flush showed, and her quickened breathing caused her breasts to rise and fall under the clinging knit.

Aware of what was happening to her and hating herself for it—even her body was betraying her with this man— Gillian seized her full lower lip between her teeth with annoyance.

And those experienced blue eyes noticed. They narrowed in a knowing, amused look. A smile twitched at the corners of his mouth. Gillian grew even hotter with rage. Maybe other women enjoyed having Burke Ferrara exercise that kind of power over them, but she, Gillian West, professor and China scholar, didn't.

As he held the hotel door for her, Gillian brushed his body lightly with hers. The cynical smile vanished, and she heard his sharp intake of breath.

So this sophisticated man wasn't immune after all. Her eyes danced. She didn't look into the question of whether she had done it subconsciously or on purpose. This arrogant Hollywood director would learn that he couldn't keep her from doing the job for which she had been hired and that she wasn't some submissive little starlet, eager to jump into his bed.

Keng was waiting beside his gray sedan. He gave Gillian a beatific smile, and they started off down the broad streets that led to downtown Peking—past the bicyclists going home from work, past the famous Peking Zoo pandas, down the wide, tree-lined Avenue of Perpetual Peace, and past the one-hundred-acre Tien -An Men Square, China's political center, and the vermilion-walled, yellow-tiled roofs of the old Forbidden City.

They sat in strained silence, the air between them electric with aroused but undischarged feelings. She was terribly aware of his long muscular leanness next to her in the car. If she was dressed for a date, he was gotten up for a night in the California hills, with a heavy sheepskin jacket, dark-blue jeans that skimmed his lean hips, and cowboy boots. But he didn't look eccentric. He was the kind of man who looked good in any kind of clothes.

From time to time she glanced at his profile. The nose jutted out confidently from the rest of the face. The upper lip was rather long, the mouth wide and well sculpted. His jaw was angular, strongly defined, powerful. He looked like a man who should be leading a wagon train west instead of directing movies.

When they finally began to talk, their conversation

was casual—chitchat about sightseeing in Peking, her flight and stopover in Japan, Chinese food. It could have been computer-programmed for a man and a woman on their way to a business conference or for strangers sharing a cab.

But underneath was the raw tension, the knowledge that they were only passing the time till an unexploded bomb went off. A ripple of fear passed through Gillian. For a moment she thought of the little college town she had left, and even of Elliot. Both so safe—and so dull.

Then Keng was pulling up outside the International Hotel. As they entered, Burke waved a hand toward the massive gilt columns in the lobby, the Chinese lanterns, with their long yellow silk tassels, and the broad stairs, carpeted in imperial red.

"This has enchantment. The new places don't." Leading her to the lobby café, with its too-few tables and its folding chairs, he said, "Looks like the set for an old Bogart movie, doesn't it?"

And it did. Utterly bored with the lack of entertainment in Peking, American, African, British, Japanese, and Arab businessmen watched one another from behind the potted palms. A sprinkling of journalists joined the game, while camera-laden tourists read week-old copies of news magazines in the bookstore and looked for postcards printed in English.

"What'll you have?" Burke asked. "They've got orange pop, Chivas Regal, apple pie à la mode, hot chocolate, coffee, tea, wine, and Tsingtao beer."

"Tea, please."

"Okay. Hold the fort. I'll be right back."

The bar was lined with thirsty people. There was one bartender on duty, wearing the unironed, unstarched, and unbleached white jacket common to service people in China. Gillian twirled an ashtray and watched the watchers at the other tables, prepared for a long wait. Then, surprisingly, Burke was there, holding a tall glass and a flowered porcelain cup with a lid.

"How'd you do it? Half the tourists in Peking must be at that bar."

"The bartender knows me. I'm a steady customer. I leave my problems behind at the White Cloud and come here."

"Don't you have a troubleshooter? Dan, for example?"

"Dan does a good job. I get the overflow." He grimaced. "The important cases."

"Is that why you left Robyn to me? She's really a big baby, you know."

Burke rolled his eyes. "You're telling me. Thousands of miles from Hollywood, and I'm stuck with an actress who's a lush. So far she hasn't come on the set under the influence. That's because I keep her scared. She hates my guts, but that's all right."

"She's pretty unhappy here."

"She knew what going on location was like. Most of our people are thrilled to be in China. She could at least be a good sport about the slight inconveniences. Temperamental actresses—I hate 'em. Thank God Andrea's not like that."

"Isn't she *ever* temperamental?"

"Only once in a while. Then watch out. When something really gets to her, she blows sky-high."

Gillian delighted in this interesting piece of information about the famous star.

"I've seen a couple of her films. She's beautiful to watch. She dropped out of films for a while, though, didn't she?"

"Yes," Burke said neutrally. "This is her comeback picture." His sapphire-blue eyes fixed her intently. "That's why, among other reasons, it has to be good. There's a lot riding on this movie—maybe the future of Chinese-American cooperation in film making, money, Andrea's future, and mine too."

For a second Gillian thought he was going to launch into his tirade against "historical crap." She stiffened and prepared to fight back. But all he said was, "You might have heard, Andrea and I were married at one time." He glanced at her left hand. "You're not, I take it."

"Divorced. Six months ago. After two years."

"It was two years for us too. I had just graduated from college, with a major in film. I made a few university-sponsored shorts and got tapped for Hollywood. I met Andrea there. She was just getting started in movies." He swirled the amber liquid around in his glass, then drank some. "Hollywood's a hard town to stay married in, no matter how much in love you are." He glanced at her finger again. "That's my excuse, anyway. What's yours?"

"No excuse." She shrugged. "We were just incompatible."

"You were the academic type and he wasn't?"

"Just the opposite," she said dryly, "if you mean the stereotype I think you do. Oh, we're both teachers, all right, but I come from one of those big, bouncy, extroverted families, whereas Elliot was the only child of elderly parents, and it showed."

"Dan told me you teach Chinese at some college in New England—how did you come to learn it?"

Gillian started to tell him what she had told Dan, when she remembered that she had explained all that in the résumé she had given Griffon Studios, one copy of which was to go to Burke Ferrara as the director she'd be working with.

"Didn't you get my résumé?"

He laughed a little, embarrassed. "I did, but I think it got deep-sixed by accident."

Gillian's eyes flashed. "I have a pretty good idea by whom."

He looked her over in his insolent, measuring way. "You should have sent a picture," he drawled. *"Then* I would have read your résumé." A grin spread across his face. "On the other hand, maybe I would just have looked at your picture."

An angry flush suffused Gillian's cheeks. This arrogant male was deliberately denigrating her as a professional person by refusing to acknowledge her as such. No doubt it was easier for his masculine pride if he saw her only in sexual terms.

Gillian rose. "I'd like to return to the hotel. May I use Keng? If not, I assure you I'm perfectly capable of taking a cab or even a bus."

Burke got up too. He put his strong hand on her bare wrist. She flinched a little, not from his strength, but from the shock waves his touch sent coursing through her. All her senses seemed to converge on that one spot where his fingers splayed themselves against her skin.

"Sit down, Gillian. You're not running from me. You're running from your oversensitive self."

"I'm not running from anything but bad manners," she retorted.

Burke bowed his head a little. "I apologize and ask for a truce. What do you say?"

"Of course," she answered coldly.

"Then sit down and tell me what was in your résumé," he coaxed.

She told him about her grandfather and how he had come to learn Chinese; her parents, both of whom were high-school teachers; her own stint at tutoring inner-city kids while she was going to college; her teaching position at Haywood; and her three months of language study in Peking the year before. She kept it all as impersonal and formal as she could, but it wasn't easy.

She felt that all the while she was feeding him these facts, he was picking up other kinds of information about her. His sensitive eyes watched intently the way she moved her body and shifted position from time to time, as well as the changes in her facial expressions and the gestures she sometimes used to emphasize her meaning. He maintained the attentive look of someone listening closely, but Gillian shrewdly guessed that it was more to hear the inflections of her voice than to absorb what she was saying.

It excited but also flustered her to receive this kind of attention from him. This sensitivity, this total awareness, was the flip side of his arrogance, a new facet of his personality, and she had an inkling that Burke Ferrara had many facets. He was more than just diamond-hard.

When she finished, he said simply, "Thank you." He drained the last of his Scotch and set the glass down decisively, then flashed that grin again.

"C'mon, let's go grab some chow. You know Peking. Choose a good place. Only, do me a favor and skip the duck joints. No pun intended." He laid the edge of his hand under his chin. "I've had Peking duck up to here. Let's get some good old American chow mein. Come to think of it, I could go for some real Maine chow. What wouldn't I give for a whole boiled lobster right now."

"But suppose *I* like duck," Gillian teased.

"You don't. No woman with your looks, brains, and wit possibly could. Come on. Let's leave the Café Whodunit before those two guys from Interpol pick us up. Pick *you* up, I mean. They've been eyeing you all night."

At Gillian's suggestion, they went to a restaurant only a ten minute walk from the International Hotel that was known to cater to individual foreigners in Peking. Most restaurants preferred large groups.

"They serve the best Mongolian hot pot in Peking," Gillian said as a waitress in a white nurse-style uniform and head scarf seated them at a table. "It's the Chinese version of a beef fondue, only it's usually made with lamb, the lobster of Inner Mongolia. Want to try it?"

"If it was good enough for Genghis Khan, it's good enough for me."

Gillian gave the order to the red-cheeked waitress, who scuttled back to the kitchen, hiding her mouth with her hand.

"I don't think I've ever really seen anybody titter before," Burke said. "I'm waiting now for the guffaws from the kitchen as she tells them about the odd couple in the dining room."

"I think she knows a little English and picked up your remark about Genghis Khan. The Chinese don't see him as the kind of monster we do. To them he's an oriental Alexander the Great, a leader who welded together the nomadic tribes of ancient Mongolia and China and created one of the world's greatest empires."

Burke took her hand in both of his. He stroked the knuckle of her right index finger with his thumb. Then his hand moved to the sensitive underside of her wrist. He lifted the heavy gold bracelet and lightly brushed the surface of her skin with his lips, sending waves of pleasure up her arm.

"How come a pretty girl like you knows so much about China? You ought to be in pictures. Come to Hollywood and I'll see what I can do about it," he said flirtatiously.

She laughed, which set their waitress giggling again as she put the sauces—soy, shrimp, pimiento, wine, bean curd, sesame seed, and others—in front of them.

"She'd make a great audience back home. Think we can get her to emigrate?" Burka asked.

"You might have to marry her."

"And eat Chinese food the rest of my life? No thanks."

Gillian showed him how to use his chopsticks, grasping the thin strips of lamb by holding the lower chopstick rigid and moving the upper one with a pincer movement. The idea was to drop the lamb in water kept boiling in a pot set over a charcoal brazier, remove it after a minute or two, and dip it in one of the sauces.

Their hands touched often, and Gillian could feel the electricity that passed between them. She realized she interested him, and she was flattered. After all, he *was* a world-famous director. But she wasn't *that* susceptible to flattery. More important, he interested *her* and secretly made her smile a little.

He was so different from other men she had known—men who weighed every word they spoke and built vast logical edifices, weaving them together with "however" and "in effect" and "on the other hand." Burke's ideas seemed to leap from one mountain peak to another like flashes of lightning. He was quick, mercurial, impatient. But underneath she sensed a steady strength, supreme self-confidence, and a masculine sureness that could all too easily become insufferable arrogance.

They walked back to the International Hotel after dinner. She shivered in the now-cold night air.

"Cold?"

"A little. But it's all right. I don't mind," she added hastily.

"I'm not going to give you my jacket," he drawled. "I told you to wear a coat."

"I wasn't hinting! You asked me a question, and I answered it."

"Next time, wear a coat," he growled.

Keng drove them back to the White Cloud, and Burke saw Gillian to her room.

"Thank you, Burke. I enjoyed the evening."

It was the truth; she had. Burke had been fascinating, witty company. But so were lots of men. And they had the advantage of not being domineering, unreasonable types she had to work with.

So she put her hand out coolly, and he took it and looked past her through the half-opened door.

"Aren't you going to ask me in for a drink of boiled water?"

She threw her head back and laughed her full, throaty laugh. Before she finished, he slid his hand under her long hair and pulled her to him. Why not? she thought. It was only a good-night kiss.

"You're irresistible when you do that," he murmured.

He lowered his mouth to hers, while his other hand went around her waist. His lips tasted firm and cool from the night air. She kissed him back lightly, then started to draw away.

But he pulled her closer. She could feel her breasts under the close-fitting knit strain against his broad chest.

His lips stroked hers in sensual sweeps that escalated her growing excitement. She quivered a little in his arms. The movement brought her into even closer contact with him. His masculine flanks pressed against her thighs, the rough denim that covered his long legs harsh against the soft knit of her dress.

As if her touch were a torch to his need, his kisses exploded against her lips. Then his smooth, gliding tongue was in her mouth, probing, exploring, taking intimate possession.

Suddenly the cold voice of common sense broke into the thrill of his embrace. The room boy might well have returned to his desk in the hall. And visitors in China who transgressed the country's strict moral code could be expelled.

"The room boy," she murmured against his lips. At the same time she tried to pull back from him.

"He's not there. I looked. Let's go into your room before he comes back."

"No! I don't want to."

It was a lie. She wanted this virile, charismatic man. But she wasn't some silly little student, to yield to a momentary passion. She hadn't gotten to be a professor at a prestigious college without showing *some* degree of maturity and self-control. And her tried-and-true judgment told her it definitely was not a good idea to get involved with Burke Ferrara. It couldn't help but complicate their working relationship, and *Siege* had been important to her from the day she had told Griffon Studios she would take the consulting job. Knowing as much as she did about the Boxer Rebellion, she didn't think she could stand seeing it depicted inaccurately.

"I think you do. Invite me in," he whispered. "I won't come unless you do."

She hesitated, and all her arguments against involvement vanished. Her hand went to her hair in the age-old gesture of a woman caught up in a sexual desire. She knew he understood the import of the movement, for in one smooth gesture he had the door open and they were inside.

For a second, in the dim light from the transom, his eyes alone made love to her as they traveled down the long line of her swanlike throat to the soft breasts peaking visibly under the clinging knit. Seeing her desirability in his eyes increased her own desire. Her tender, pliant body reached out for his. She swayed a little, and his strong arms captured her again. His mouth covered hers in passionate, hungry kisses. When he finally let her go, she was breathless. She stepped back, her breasts heaving with the feelings he had aroused.

He watched her, a lazy, sensual half-smile playing around his lips. Slowly, negligently, his eyes feasted on her graceful neck, her straight shoulders, the soft flesh that ended in the upward sweep of her breasts under the knit top, the curving hips, and long, shapely legs. His blue eyes were warm with admiration and narrowed with arousal. He took a step toward her, whispering, "Lovely, lovely Gillian."

An awareness of what she was doing washed over her. She backed away. But she was still shaken by desire, and self-control was coming hard. The result was that she couldn't manage to get out what she wanted to say— a sort of no-fault, friendly statement that this was as far as she wanted to go.

Instead she found herself saying in glacial tones, "Please go, Mr. Ferrara."

It sounded so ridiculous, so Victorian, she could have cried with frustration. She knew from his eyes that it immediately put her in one of those high-necked, mutton-sleeved dresses that went with that kind of dialogue.

But he didn't laugh, although that might almost have been better. Instead his eyes hardened into glittering blue stones. Muttering, "I didn't think you were a tease, Gillian," he advanced on her in one long, stalking movement. He ran his hands over her hair and down her shoulders before he pulled her in to him, so close this time she was almost overpowered by his masculine hardness.

His mouth was hot and bruising now. She twisted her face away, but with one firm hand on her jaw he brought it back to him. Then he softened his kiss, working his lips against hers in provocative movements that drove her wild with longing for something more. She heard herself uttering questioning little moans as she parted her lips under the pressure of his and sought the soft strokings of his tongue.

All the while his fingertips were lightly moving the knit material of her top against the flesh underneath, exciting the sensory nerves of her skin to a point of delicious anticipation. She moved seductively against him and thrilled anew to the hard, muscular feel of this magnificent male.

A warm, sweet languor flowed through her. She gave herself up to the kisses that rained on her eyelids, the points of her cheekbones, and under the clean line of her jaw. She bent her head back so his lips could reach the places his eyes had so hotly desired moments before.

Her eyes closed, she was in the Tunnel of Love with this attractive man. His kisses were waking her up to a world of feelings she had almost forgotten about. She didn't want it to stop—ever. And in a slow-moving tango of bodies pressed one to the other, they moved toward the bed.

Just then they heard someone rattling away in Chinese outside her door.

"The room boys!" Gillian said.

"So?"

"What if they saw you?"

"What if they did?"

"We could be expelled for immoral conduct. Then where would your film be?"

He smiled. "I'm not worried."

She was still in his arms. He bent his lips to hers again, but she pulled back sharply. The interruption had given her time to think. She realized anew that her work and Burke Ferrara just wouldn't mix. And she was choosing between them—right now.

"Even so, I think you should leave," she said, stepping away from him.

"You'll clutch at any excuse, won't you? I hoped I could melt that New England ice, but it's thicker than I thought." His vivid blue eyes burned with contempt. His voice was low-pitched and angry. "Next time, lady historical consultant, you'll beg me to stay."

The sarcasm implicit in "lady historical consultant" restored Gillian completely to herself. She had earned her honors in the academic world against severe competition, most of it male. And her level of tolerance for being patronized by macho men was zero.

"That's a gauntlet I don't care to pick up, Mr. Ferrara, especially since it really belongs on the floor." She turned to go back to the living room of her suite. "Please feel free to stay till it's safe to leave."

"I'm dying of fear!"

"In any case, I guess you can let yourself out. See you on the set tomorrow?" she added sweetly.

His sea-captain's eyes snapped with anger. "Right. But if you think you can keep me out of your bed *and* screw up my film, you've got a whole new box of guesses coming."

She heard the door close behind her and sank into one of the dingy armchairs. Her heart was pounding wildly, her emotions a confused welter of frustrated desire and relief. There was no way, absolutely none, she told herself, that she would go to bed with Burke Ferrara. It was bad business to sleep with a man you worked with, or, in this case, worked against, she thought with a wry twist of her mouth. And they weren't in love; there was only this strong, surging attraction between them. For all she knew, he might even have been softening her up so she'd be less trouble on the set. A man as sophisticated as

Burke Ferrara might not think twice about such a maneuver.

But later as she lay in bed, taut as a violin string from his touch, her mouth still warm from his kisses, she wondered seriously if she'd be able to resist him. And if not, *then* what would happen to her work? Would she be less critical of what he did with *Siege?*

chapter 3

GILLIAN WOKE UP in the morning with all her natural high spirits and zest for life intact, no bitter residue from last night's date with Burke, no sour taste of regret. She had done the right thing. What was more, she was in ever-fascinating China, she was involved in making a movie, and today she would meet Burke Ferrara on the field of combat.

Excited by the day's prospects, she sprang out of bed, raised the window sash, and did ten pushups. You couldn't consort with famous actors and directors and bulge like a bagel. This was Hollywood, baby, not Haywood College, where all anyone wanted to know was the topic of your dissertation.

She selected as work clothes a rust-colored sweater and gray flannel pants suit, and pinned her hair up in a businesslike chignon. When she got to the dining room on the main floor, she whispered a few words to the waitress and was directed to a large empty table in the rear of the room on the side occupied by people Gillian recognized as belonging to the *Siege* cast and crew.

Gillian was still eating her breakfast, drinking warm, sweet yogurt soup and deftly popping thin little slices of fried pork into her mouth with chopsticks, when Andrea Steele came up to her table.

The actress introduced herself and said, "But why are you eating all alone?"

Gillian laughed. "This is the table the hotel staff has set aside for guests who want the Chinese, rather than the Western, breakfast. And rice porridge with soy sauce and dried fish and tea aren't exactly popular items."

She stared for a moment with frank curiosity at the woman who now sat down beside her. At thirty-five, Andrea Steele had the kind of ripe beauty that had led the great painters to pose their mistresses as the goddess Venus. Her full-breasted figure was statuesque and perfectly proportioned, her eyes large and violet-hued. Dark hair set off the milky, still-smooth skin. But most of her beauty lay in the exquisite bone structure of her face—the shapely nose, high cheekbones, and sloping planes that led to a prominent, but not overpowering, jaw. Andrea Steele was the kind of woman who would still be lovely at sixty.

Her voice was modulated and low, totally lacking in any regional accent—all, obviously, the result of training. She was playing the role of hostess now, welcoming the new arrival, but her manner was simple and natural, not oozing with forced graciousness.

This beautiful, charming woman had been Burke Ferrara's wife. Was it possible, Gillian wondered, that he had given her up forever, especially now that they were working together? And if he hadn't, what was he doing making love to her, Gillian, last night?

"This is late for me," Andrea was saying now, her eyes following the sleight-of-hand Gillian was executing with her chopsticks. "I'm usually on the set at the crack of dawn to be costumed and made up, but Burke thought I had earned an extra hour's sleep today."

Gillian gave her a speculative look. There had been an unmistakable lilt in her voice when she mentioned Burke, and her lovely, clear eyes had become brighter.

"He's so considerate!" Andrea went on.

"Considerate" was the last word Gillian would have applied to Burke Ferrara. Her eyebrows shot up at the very idea.

The dark-fringed violet eyes were watching her narrowly. With a little laugh, Andrea amended her statement. "Oh, he can be tough, too, but"—she waved a graceful white hand in the air—"let's face it, Burke and I have a special relationship." With her eyes still on Gillian, Andrea added, "Very special."

An unexpected twinge of jealousy shot through Gillian like a sharp physical pain. The morsel of steamed roll with plum filling she had in her mouth had suddenly become hard to swallow. But she smiled politely and kept her eyes steady.

Then she mentally kicked herself for reacting as she had. Of course Andrea and Burke had a "special relationship." So did she and Elliot. Once you'd been married to a man, it was a little hard thereafter to regard him as just your ordinary, average man in the street. But this thought was followed by another, less comforting one. More than the memory of a friendly divorce was indicated here. Andrea was definitely sending her a "Hands Off, He's Mine" message.

Like a fan at a tennis match, Gillian then watched the ball return to the first court. Andrea might have a "very special" relationship with Burke, but it wasn't one she was sure of, or she wouldn't be warning Gillian off. Undoubtedly she had learned of Burke's date with Gillian the previous evening.

Andrea unexpectedly rose. "If you'll excuse me, Gillian, I'll join Burke. If I don't, the poor dear will have to eat alone." She smiled. "See you on the set."

What Andrea had meant by "alone" was hard to understand, inasmuch as there were two other people at the table with Burke. Gillian hadn't noticed him come in, but Andrea evidently had—and too quickly, for someone who wasn't watching.

He looked up as Andrea approached, then past her at Gillian. She flushed to be caught staring at him like that and lifted her chin a little, defiantly, to offset the trip hammer of her heart.

The proud set of his head, those arresting blue eyes, sky-bright this morning against the tanned face, and the sweep of that mobile, emotional mouth were sending waves of deliciously painful excitement through her.

She smiled a little to herself at the clothes he had on. A worn flannel shirt, its plaids muted by many washings, stretched across his broad chest, showing his strong brown neck where the top button was undone. Did he have any new clothes? she wondered.

Then, as she might have expected, he gave her a polite nod coupled with the sardonic smile he seemed to reserve for her alone. Andrea must have seen it too, because she turned her head quickly and sent a searching look Gillian's way. Then she gracefully lowered herself into the chair Burke held out for her. She brought her beautiful face close to his and laid her hand on his arm in a proprietary way.

During the next few days Gillian met the rest of the cast and some of the many people involved in making *Siege*—the production managers and assistant directors, the director of photography and his camera crew, the dressers and makeup artists, the set decorator, and others. Chinese technicians eager to learn Western methods also worked on the production, and Chinese artisans created most of the costumes and sets.

Gillian watched the daily takes with absorbed interest. The young Marine lieutenant was being played by Trent Baylor, son of a famous actor and a real pro. He never became temperamental on the set, needed little rehearsing, and hardly ever blew his lines.

He was as cool off the set as on. Friendly with everyone, he steered clear of the usual romantic involvements and power-seeking alliances. Between takes he methodically worked his way through a stack of crossword-puzzle books that he had brought with him.

Phil Grossman, Burke's director of photography, was just the opposite of the Cold Fish, as Robyn called Trent Baylor. Phil was a warm-hearted bear of a man with curly red hair and a red beard, and sad eyes, which seemed incongruous in the midst of all that color.

The Chinese were fascinated by him, and it was generally agreed among cast and crew that Phil collected bigger crowds than any of them. His bright hair could often be seen above a sea of darker heads as he took a Polaroid picture of some apple-cheeked fat baby in quilted clothes and, after a few suspense-filled minutes, handed the snapshot to the shyly smiling mother, or photographed a child wide-eyed with fear and wonder.

The children who lived on the street outside the hotel compound waited for him to return from work every afternoon. Then, chattering and bright-eyed, they would gather around him while he did magic tricks for them, pulling multicolored handkerchiefs out of his sleeve and ping-pong balls from behind their ears.

The tricks were so transparent, Gillian doubted that even the children were fooled. But they always came, and Phil never failed them even when there were dark circles of fatigue under his somber blue eyes. Gillian guessed that the magic that existed between the children and Phil Grossman had nothing to do with parlor tricks at all.

Once, as Gillian and Robyn passed the usual cluster of children and the red-bearded man, Robyn said a little wistfully, "That Phil's a nice guy."

Gillian stared at her, surprised. Robyn never had a good word to say for anybody. Burke was the "Dictator,"

Andrea (in Robyn's sarcastic tone) the "Great Star," Dan Ross a "surf bum," Trent Baylor a "handsome hunk of ice."

"The kids love him," Gillian answered. "And you're right, he *is* a nice guy. But he never looks really happy."

"He lost his wife and two kids in one of those big California forest fires. Phil wasn't there; he was on location somewhere. Their house seemed safe, so the wife and kids weren't evacuated, but the fire jumped, as it will sometimes, and they never had a chance to get out. I guess the poor guy's been looking for kids to love ever since."

And a woman? Gillian wondered.

Since the day Gillian had gone to her room, Robyn had treated her as a friend—her only one. Toward everyone else she displayed a belligerent, chip-on-the-shoulder attitude, which, Gillian guessed, was defensive in origin.

Although Robyn had been acting a long time, she had never progressed beyond secondary roles, stereotyped character parts, mostly of a dizzy blonde, and it looked as though she might not be getting even those parts much longer.

Even Gillian could see that Robyn's work was deteriorating day to day. She always showed up on the set sober, but her behavior often revealed the effects of heavy drinking. She would fluff lines, appearing vague and unable to concentrate, or fail to understand what Burke wanted from her in a scene. The director and the actress seemed locked into a cycle of her failure and his disapproval, followed by renewed efforts at patience on his part, efforts that would suddenly give way to exasperated, shouted criticism.

Still, watching Burke work, Gillian developed, against her will, a new respect for him. It was a difficult job, using other people as an artist uses paint, and a writer, words, to tell a story or realize an idea. Even before rehearsing a scene, Burke worked with his actors, probing characters' motivations for their behavior in the story. Then his long narrow hands would shape in the air the kind of movements he wanted from them. His clever, animated face would assume the expressions they were supposed to show. And he would move around the set with pantherlike grace, acting out the scene.

When he rehearsed Andrea, an almost religious hush invariably fell upon the set. Cast and crew watched as if mesmerized. The communication between the two was so immediate and sure, the impression was that of two stars of the ballet performing a pas de deux.

Did they see each other after work? Hard as she tried to keep it out of her mind, the question tantalized Gillian. She told herself repeatedly there was no reason for her to care if they did. She certainly had no intention of going out with Burke Ferrara again. Not that there was much likelihood of it. It was all they could do to be civil to each other on the set.

Highly aware of her commitment to the film studio, she watched each scene closely for mistakes. But there were none for a while, and she was glad. Burke made no secret of his contempt for the "lady historical consultant," the meddlesome professor who busied herself with unimportant details. So it wouldn't take much, Gillian thought, for any discussion they might have to become heated. Moreover, the memory of their passionate embraces still lay like a firebrand between them when they met. At times she could feel his eyes flicking over her in a way that left no doubt about his interest—and its nature.

The dividing line between the heat of hate and the heat of amorous passion could be a narrow one. But if you exercised caution, Gillian told herself, you could always avoid the flames that licked at your senses. That was something her Puritan ancestors had known very well—with the possible exception, Gillian thought with a rueful lift of her eyebrows, of one Abigail West, who had been hanged for receiving nocturnal visits from the devil. So when Burke invited her to have a drink with

him at the International Café after they had finished
shooting a scene nearby, she politely refused.

He drew his brows together in that familiar black line.
"It's strictly business," he said dryly. "There are some
scenes I want to discuss with you. I thought I'd get around
to it during the day, but I'm always too busy."

"Can't Dan make these explanations?"

He narrowed his eyes in the way he had that spelled
danger. "If I had wanted Dan to do it, I would have said
so," he growled.

With a shrug she fell into step with him, walking along
the long, busy streets that led to the hotel. The steady
pedaling of bicyclists went on as usual. Street cleaners
in white gauze face masks pushed utensil carts and swept
the gutters with sorghum brooms. Large, modern buses
went by, crammed with blue and gray tunics.

They didn't talk, yet the silence wasn't oppressive.
Gillian could tell from the absorbed look on Burke's face,
the way he ran his hands through his thick brown hair,
rubbed his chin pensively, that he was going over in his
mind the scenes he had shot that day, the ones he would
do tomorrow, the amount of rehearsing that would be
necessary, places where he could cut corners.

She thought about him, about the kind of man he was,
about his relationships with the people they both knew.
Then she brought herself up short. Curiosity was a dangerous sign. Next she'd be wondering what he did with
the ties he got for Christmas, where he went for vaca-
tions, whether he wore pajamas or slept in the raw—the
silly things that meant you really had fallen for someone.

The bar was as crowded as usual. While Burke went
to get their drinks, Gillian watched the people at the
tables around her. When her eyes met those of a man
who suddenly appeared, smiling, at her table, she started
in surprise.

"Hello, Gillian. Remember me?"

"Paul Rogers!" she gasped. "What are you doing in

China?" She surveyed the neat, symmetrical features before her, the carefully brushed ash-blond hair. Paul hadn't changed a bit in the four years since she had last seen him. "Please—sit down."

"I'm working as a consultant for an American business firm in Peking. I quit teaching a year after I left Haywood, and went to California, you know."

"I didn't know that. How's Lorraine?"

"She split while we were still in San Francisco. She joined one of those fruit-and-nut cults and slapped a bumper sticker—'Happiness Is Being Happy'—on her car to celebrate it. Our mailman, who had his doctorate in anthro but couldn't get a job in his field, saw the bumper sticker and, it turned out, was a member of the same cheery cult. This gave Lorraine somebody a lot easier to relate to than a gloom-and-doom economist like yours truly, plus there was the fact that he was younger, more hedonistic, to use the ultimate in euphemisms, and was earning almost as much as I was. I don't know when the mail got delivered while they were playing post office, but nobody could say they weren't happy. Anyway, she left, he got another route, and I moved to L. A. and ended up here." Paul glanced toward the bar. "What's taking Elliot so long?"

"I'm not here with Elliot, Paul. We were divorced six months ago."

"Is that so? I had no idea. I'm sorry."

"No need to be."

"So we're in the same boat." Paul had a gleam in his eye that wasn't entirely unfamiliar. Even when they were both still married, he had made a pass at her once or twice at faculty parties.

"I suppose so," she said noncommittally. It was nice to see somebody from home, but she didn't think she wanted to take the relationship beyond that point of auld lang syne. Not that Paul wasn't attractive. That blond hair above horn-rimmed glasses and a certain quizzical smile had caused many a flutter among the women stu-

dents at Haywood. "I'm here with a friend," she continued. "He's still at the bar."

"I see. Well, what are *you* doing in Peking, Gillian?
Brushing up on your Chinese?"

Gillian shook her head. "I'm the historical consultant
on an American film being shot here."

"You are? Good for you! Any chance of our getting
together?" He surveyed the bar again quickly. "Or are
you all tied up?"

"Not in the least."

"Wonderful! I'm here at the International. I live above
the store, so to speak. What with Peking's being short
of office space, my firm's rented a suite in the hotel. I
was thinking of doing some shopping in the Street of
Antiques tomorrow. If you can get away, give me a call.
Here's my number." He handed her a business card. "But
if not, I'll call you and we'll go out some evening soon.
Where are you staying?"

"The White Cloud."

Paul nodded. "A good hotel, and quieter than the
International." He glanced at his watch. "Listen, I'm
supposed to take some visiting firemen to the Peking
Opera tonight." He squeezed her hand affectionately.
"I've got to go, but I'm delighted you're here, Gillian."
He gave her a significant look. "And without Elliot."

She didn't have time for a reply. Burke was setting
two glasses down on the table and boasting, "Didn't spill
a drop" at the same time that his eyes pierced Paul like
steel-blue stilettos.

Gillian introduced the two men and was amused to
see that Paul became a little flustered upon meeting the
famous director.

"May I buy you a drink?" Burke said gruffly.

"No, thanks," Paul answered in his light, precise voice.
"I have an appointment I must keep." He got up and said
to Gillian, "Remember, keep an evening open for me."

Gillian smiled. "I hope you enjoy the opera."

Paul grimaced. "I'll try."

"Who's your scholarly-looking friend?" Burke asked as he slipped into Paul's place.

"A former professor at Haywood. He moved to California and lost his wife to the mailman."

"That figures. The mailman probably delivered."

Gillian smiled into her up-tilted glass. Could Burke be jealous?

"What's he doing here?" This was asked in a disinterested tone.

"Consulting for an American firm."

"Who's educating the youth of America while all you professorial types are running around China?"

She only smiled at him, and he started talking about a scene he wanted to shoot in a few days. It was the entry into Peking by the Allied forces sent to raise the siege of the legations. And to Gillian's surprise, he was asking her advice about it.

They sat at the table exchanging ideas, and though they didn't always agree, for the first time Burke showed he respected her knowledge of the period. They were even relaxed enough with each other to joke about their differences.

Why couldn't he always be like this? Gillian thought. This was the way she had expected her job to be, a situation based on the free exchange of ideas between equals.

By the time they had finished their business, the crowd at the bar had thinned out. Burke went back for another Scotch for himself and a glass of white wine for Gillian.

Alone at the table, she stared, unseeing, at a rubber plant with yellowing leaves. Meeting Paul Rogers again had brought back memories of Elliot. She raised an ironic eyebrow. Their marriage might have worked in China, where a one-child family was the ideal. Elliot had been an ardent believer in population control. Even the single child to which he had insisted they limit themselves had been scheduled for later, when they were both firmly established in their academic careers. And Elliot had worried so much about Gillian's getting pregnant even on the pill that he had been a cautious, unsatisfactory lover. Actually, though, Gillian mused, love making reflected your personality as surely as your toothpaste habits did, and Elliot fussily measured out both.

It hadn't been just sex, either, that was wrong with their marriage. She discovered after a while that they had everything in common but the important things. They both liked books, music, the theater, long walks, cross-country skiing. They shared the same tastes but were as far apart emotionally as two people could be.

Elliot's field was Latin and classical Greek. What else could he have studied but dead languages? He had grown up in the middle house of three big white frame ones with black-green shutters on an elm-lined street in a decaying New England city. The other two were occupied by maiden aunts and uncles, who regarded Elliot, the first child in the family for many years, with a mixture of awe and detached curiosity.

His parents were grazing fifty when he was born. The child was like a moon rock, to be handled with long tongs and protective gloves. Gillian eventually understood that people really were like inhabitants of another planet to him. Since he was studious but not introspective, that included himself. He knew from his reading of the Latin poets that emotion and passion existed. But he experienced them in a highly diluted form which he thought was the way other people felt too.

Gillian's enthusiasm and playfulness, her open expression of her feelings, and her passion in bed frightened him. What she had once thought were his virtues appeared in a different light when she got to know him better. His sensitivity was one-sided; his widely professed love of learning, egotistical ambition; his love for her, simply the desire for a conventionally appropriate mate.

Why had she married him? Once she fell out of love,

she honestly didn't know. Six months after her divorce, she still felt as though she had just been let out of prison.

Gillian was moodily tracing her initials on the table with the Scotch that had slopped out of Burke's first drink when he returned.

"Homesick?" he asked, setting the drinks down.

"Not really. Seeing Paul brought back memories, that's all."

"Of your ex-husband?"

Gillian nodded. "I suppose everyone goes through the same syndrome after a divorce—wondering if she could have tried harder, done better."

"And what answer do you come up with?"

She thought a while, still drawing the *G*. Then she raised her head. "To be quite frank, I think Elliot probably shouldn't have married at all, but since he did, it shouldn't have been me."

"That's looking at it from his point of view. How do you feel about what the marriage did to you?"

"You know," she said slowly, "the last time I saw Elliot in our house, he was packing to move out. He had gotten an apartment near the college and had moved everything but his books. He couldn't find one of his Latin books, a collection of the plays of Terence. He became very upset, accused me of having hidden it, and wouldn't leave without it even though he had to make a Boston-to-New York flight to attend a meeting. I offered to look for it while he was gone, but he refused.

"While he was ranting and raving, rummaging through the house and making a nuisance of himself, I ran through the gamut of emotions. First I thought it was funny, then I pitied him, then I was disgusted. Finally I thought that if he didn't stop, I'd either go out of my mind or kill him. To get rid of him, I ended up taking all the books out of all the bookcases, and I found the damn book. It had been right under his nose all that time."

"I hope you threw it at him," Burke said angrily.

"I should have, but you just didn't do that kind of thing with Elliot." Gillian wondered if Burke could understand that.

"Why'd you ever marry a guy like that?"

"I thought I loved him and that we had a lot in common. But we didn't."

"And you couldn't have found that out before?" Burke probed.

"Not really. It was only after I was married that I started examining myself and my feelings. That's when I became fully conscious of myself as a woman."

As soon as she heard her own words, she regretted them. He was running his eyes over her now in that insolently seductive way that annoyed her at the same time that it made her feel soft and weak inside.

She bent her head and started retracing the *G*. He took her finger and kissed it, then licked it clean with his tongue and gave it a final nibble that made her senses sharp with excitement. She wondered what he'd do next.

"I'd say you were quite a woman, Gillian."

He opened her palm then and brushed his lips across its soft center. Her own lips parted. She moistened them with her tongue and half-closed her large deep-brown eyes, giving herself over to the electrifying touches of his lips on her skin.

She was safe from him and from her own desire, she thought, so long as they stayed in the café. But people were waiting for their table, and they had finished their drinks. Burke laid a hand on her arm silently, and she got up and led the way out of the room.

There was no place for them to go but the car driven by Keng. Burke slammed shut the semi-opaque glass divider that separated chauffeur from passengers and enveloped Gillian in his arms. His mouth covered hers, and his lips moved restlessly back and forth, seeking something with passionate impatience. At the same time his hand moved under her jacket and set up the delicious friction of her silk blouse against her skin. The crush of his lips on hers, the push of his tongue into her mouth, and the pungent male smell of him awakened fires of passion that raced through her, burning away all resolve to resist him. Her hunger for him drew her arms in a curving circle around his broad shoulders and across the firm muscles of his back.

He lifted his mouth only once, to whisper her name. "Gillian." It sounded like an incantation to a love goddess.

Then his mouth sought her delicately molded cheekbones, her closed eyelids, and small chin. He let her long hair cover them like a waterfall while he nuzzled the nape of her neck and caressed it, nibbling it a little, tickling it with his tongue, and finally kissing it.

From there his lips traced a path along the pulsing vein of her throat to the sensitive hollow at its base. A thrilling, tingling warmth stole over her. She arched her back, holding herself out to him.

He undid the buttons of her silk shirt, slowly because they were small, while her senses screamed for him to go faster. His hands finally slid inside her shirt and bra. His fingers glided to her waiting breasts. Under his passionate cupping touch, their softness was reshaped into the palm of his hands.

Her breath quickened with yearning, and she didn't care. She was losing herself in him, conscious only of him, the feel of him, the scent of him, her desire to know him physically, intimately.

A truck horn—long, strident, aggressively annoying—gradually restored her to the world outside. She sat up and started to button her blouse. She wanted to pull completely away from Burke, but he wouldn't let her go.

"You're freezing up on me, aren't you?" he said.

Gillian tried to sound calm and unflustered. "I don't usually make love in the back seat of a car."

"No? Where *do* you usually make love, then?" His eyes sparkled mischievously.

"That's my business," she said firmly.

"I don't think so. I think it's mine. That's twice now you've let me melt you up to a point. Then you've made a mad dash back to the freezer. What gives? I know you want me"—his voice became husky—"and God knows I want you."

She pushed him away from her and retreated to the far corner of the car.

"I don't go in for fun and games with the boss," she said, making her voice flat and colorless.

"I don't think you go in for fun and games with any-body. I think you've been in school too long, Miss West."

She fought back the impulse to take up his taunting challenge, to show him the kind of woman she was. But that would only be playing his game. All she'd get out of it would be a few nights of pleasure, followed by the feeling that she had been cheap. So their good nights were stiff and cold. In the dim light of the corridor outside her door, his eyes, darkened by hostility again, were almost navy, and his mouth was a ruler-straight, angry line.

But when she lay in bed that night, she ran her fingers across her cheekbones and lips and chin, over her shoulders and down her sides, and lightly on her breasts—all the places where he had touched or kissed her. She re-called the almost-fierce look on his hawklike face, his hungry blue eyes, the taste of his mouth and tongue, and the strong but sensitive way his hands touched her.

Everything about him intrigued her, called to her, compelled her. His well-shaped head, his aquiline fea-tures, his tall, rangy build—all answered some precon-ceived idea she had, some archetypal image buried deep in her subconscious, of what she wanted her man to be.

She fell asleep thinking of him. Some time later she woke up to a soft but persistent knocking at her door.

chapter 4

EVEN AT THREE o'clock in the morning, Andrea Steel was a vision of loveliness. Her hair was a night-dark cloud around her chiseled features; her eyes a deep wood-violet in the pale face. And her diaphanous gown and peignoir, patterned with large pastel flowers, subtly suggested the full womanly beauty beneath.

"I couldn't sleep," she said simply in that low, modulated voice of hers. "I thought perhaps you might have a sleeping pill."

Gillian's eyes opened wide. She felt she needed a little time to take all this in. Did people knock on one another's doors in the middle of the night in Hollywood to ask for a sleeping pill? Or did the sleepless Andrea have something else in mind? "I don't use them." Gillian laughed. "I barely get my head on the pillow before I conk out." She looked doubtfully behind her into the room. "But I could make you a cup of tea. Would that help?"

It wouldn't, Gillian thought immediately afterward. It couldn't. Tea was a stimulant, not a soporific. But from the pleased look on Andrea's face, the actress either didn't know this or didn't care. So Gillian ushered Andrea into her little suite.

She spooned green tea leaves into two cups and poured hot water over them from the big, gaudily flowered thermos that sat on the floor. All the time, she was fighting off a fit of the giggles. Mentally she prepared a magazine article: "What Andrea Steele Told Me Over the Tea Leaves at 3:00 A. M. in Peking."

Every once in a while she stole a glance at Andrea. The actress sat like a classical statue, hands loosely clasped in her lap, her robe draped gracefully over her regal form.

"Andrea, your tea's ready," Gillian said softly.

The violet eyes looked into Gillian's sleepy brown ones, and Andrea stretched out a graceful hand for the cup.

After a delicate sip Andrea fixed Gillian again with her eyes. "Dan tells me you and Burke have had a few, shall we say, close encounters."

Gillian was shocked by the abruptness of the attack. Gone was the Olympian remoteness. Gillian faced instead a cold, appraising look coupled with a saccharine smile.

Her first impulse was to tell Andrea it was none of her business, but curiosity about what Andrea could tell *her* led Gillian to shrug and say noncommittally, "There are always scenes to be discussed—historical details, interpretation of events, and so on."

"Of course." Andrea studied Gillian over her teacup. Her eyes roved over the tailored pajamas and travel robe, the worn sandals Gillian preferred to slippers, the toenails—without polish, a pale mother-of-pearl.

"Burke is a highly sophisticated man, a Hollywood man, if you will. He isn't"—the gentle voice hesitated, but the eyes glittered hard as amethysts—"for everyone. Just any woman, I mean."

"Have you come to warn me of something or to call me 'just any woman,' Andrea?"

The slight trembling she could hear in her own voice annoyed Gillian. It didn't come from fear. Gillian had gotten over her awe of the great movie star. Watching her work every day, learning her lines, building her performance, and criticizing herself in the daily showing of the rushes had made Andrea very human to her.

But Gillian was mad. And she wasn't an actress, so she couldn't control her voice or use her facial muscles to hide rather than show her feelings.

"I don't want to see you get hurt, that's all," Andrea claimed.

Gillian clamped her lips firmly over the vulgar epithet that threatened to escape them at that blatant bit of hypocrisy. She didn't want an open quarrel with Andrea. That would make her work even more difficult than it already was.

"That's very kind of you but totally unnecessary. To reiterate, my relationship with Burke is purely professional. If it's your business . . . ?" she added with a slightly questioning inflection.

"Burke and I were married once. The kind of feeling we had for each other never really dies. We will always be each other's business."

The palpable truth of this statement struck Gillian like a blow in the solar plexus. What Andrea said was evident in the delicacy with which Burke directed his star, in her quick apprehension of what he wanted almost before he told her, even in their easy camaraderie on the set.

And yet . . . and yet. Gillian's hand flew to her mouth. The touch of her fingers against her lips brought back the pressure of his firm mouth on hers, the tingling as their lips came together, the deep sensual response as his tongue hotly invaded her waiting mouth. Under the boyish blue cotton pajamas, her breasts rose a little and her body relaxed at the memory of those long, supple fingers and the joy they had given her.

She lifted her chin. Her soft brown eyes took fire from her anger and her determination. If she decided not to become involved with Burke Ferrara, it would be *her* choice, not a decision dictated to her by someone else, even the great Andrea Steele, movie star and ex-wife.

Andrea watched her, the lavender eyes almost completely hidden under the chiseled lids. The sweet, good-friend smile was gone. Her knuckles were white on the carved wooden armrests. The nails of one hand dug into the dingy fabric.

"I'm accustomed to choosing my friends as I wish, not as another person decides." Gillian stood. "If you've finished your tea...I don't want to hurry you, but it is late and we have to work tomorrow."

Andrea rose in one graceful movement and handed her cup to Gillian. Her eyes were wide with sorrow now, her arched brows drawn together in a worried little pucker.

"Be careful, dear. Love's a dangerous game. I don't think they teach that in college."

"Not per se. On the other hand, there are courses in acting—both on screen and off."

Instantly the mask was gone. A look of murderous hate contorted Andrea's lovely features, then vanished. Her face smooth again, she went to the door.

"I know you won't mention this little talk to Burke." Her eyes widened with false sincerity. "It would be so...so pointless."

Gillian stared at the closed door, her mind a kaleidoscope of confusing thoughts. All her bravado was gone now. She wasn't sure what was the truth and what wasn't. Perhaps Burke was, as Andrea said, a Hollywood man, one whose interest in Gillian had been only sexual curiosity, the urge to discover what making love to an intellectual would be like. Maybe it was true that he and Andrea would always belong to each other—to stray at times, try other partners, divorce, and perhaps remarry, but always be the two halves that made one.

Suddenly an image of Burke's lean, muscular torso clasping Andrea's milky white statuesque form came into her mind, and Gillian thrust it savagely from her.

But why did she even care? a slightly weary voice within her asked. Who wanted a superior-acting, hot-tempered Hollywood director anyway? It was asking for trouble. Hadn't she had enough of that with Elliot?

As she went back to bed and pulled the clean, tattle-gray sheets up to her chin, Gillian reflected that there were different kinds of trouble. With Elliot life had been a desert landscape littered with the bleached bones of dead emotions, a dead land unwatered by love—a cactus land.

What would a life with Burke be like? Smiling, Gillian drifted off to sleep without answering that question.

The next morning the lobby was a mini-crowd scene. Members of the film company milled around impatiently, waiting for the bus driver who would take them to the Forbidden City for the day's filming, and the driver was late. Fortunately Burke wasn't in the crowd, so the tension that had gripped Gillian since breakfast left her. She had made her decision in the cool gray hours of early morning. She would be courteous when they met, and even friendly in an impersonal sort of way—a working colleague, that was all. She also knew that the less she saw of him, the easier it would be to stick to her decision.

Andrea wasn't there either, but that wasn't unusual. The stars of *Siege* left early in a special limousine, to be made up and costumed in the dressing trailers on the set. Burke could have used a car too, but he insisted he could pick up "vibes" and assess morale better if he rode the bus with everyone else. Gillian had to admit Burke was democratic, although when it came to Liberty, Equality, and Fraternity, he was most apt to adhere to the third.

Gillian started to make her way to Robyn, then saw that Phil Grossman was cutting a swathe through the crowd in the same direction. She hung back and watched, amazed, as Robyn smiled shyly up at the big man and he beamed down at her.

Robyn St. Regis *shy?* Gillian looked again to see if she was putting on an act. But there was no mistaking the import of the smiles, the lowered eyes, even the girlish blush.

She realized then that Robyn even looked different. The circles under her eyes were gone. Her skin glowed with health. All her latent prettiness had surfaced, and she looked years younger.

Gillian whistled softly under her breath. Robyn was in love! And from the way he was looking at her, Phil returned her affection. Smiling, Gillian turned away. At that moment she saw Burke taking the marble lobby steps two at a time.

His eyes swept over the crowd, then rested on her. Rudely, imperiously, he started to elbow his way through to her as though the seconds before he could be by her side actually counted. With her heart beating fast at the sight of him and her color high, Gillian tried to escape, but the crowd was all around her, and she couldn't move.

At that moment Phil stopped Burke and spoke to him earnestly for a minute or two. Burke listened, his hands jammed deep in the pockets of his sheepskin jacket. Then, pushing his corduroy cap to the back of his head, he used his hands to illustrate the answer to Phil's question.

The lobby was echoing now with high-pitched conversation as people tried to pass the time with chatter and gossip. When a Chinese appeared at the door, all eyes turned toward him and the room fell silent.

With a distressed look the man started speaking in his own language.

"What's he saying?" Dan asked Gillian.

Raising her voice so that everyone could hear, Gillian translated the driver's words. "He was in an accident. He was riding his bicycle here when a bus cut in front of him. He was thrown from his bike. Other bicyclists stopped to help, and a doctor examined him and said he was all right. The wind was knocked out of him, but he wasn't hurt. And he's very sorry to be late."

"In L. A. he'd still be lying on the freeway," someone said.

"In L. A. he wouldn't be on the freeway. Not on a bike."

"Hell, no, he'd be driving his own car."

As the crowd surged toward the door, Gillian was carried along to where Burke was waiting for her. Looking at his sheepskin jacket, Gillian bent her head to hide a smile. If Californians thought *this* was cold . . . !

"What's the joke?" He looked down at her morosely. "You look as though you just blew into town from Outer Mongolia."

"That's where the studio will be sending me if I don't bring this picture in on time." As they started to follow the crowd, he asked, "Did you see Andrea this morning?"

For a second Gillian thought he knew about Andrea's 3:00 A. M. visit to her room.

Then he went on. "I had an early breakfast with her. She seemed jumpy. I thought you might know what's eating her. You know, woman-to-woman stuff."

"Right. We all have antennas for just that sort of thing. Actually, you and Andrea seem close enough. I should think *you* would know." Then, furious with herself, she watched that lazy smile spread across his lips and his sea-blue eyes gleam with amusement.

He gripped her arm above the elbow and pulled her nearer to him. "I believe in close relations, don't you, China Girl?"

"I think the bus is leaving."

Dan came back just then to get them. He stopped in the doorway and stared at Burke and Gillian. Then he smiled and raised his eyebrows.

"You two coming?"

I can see the item in the gossip columns now, Gillian

thought. "What well-known director is shooting his own love scenes in the People's Republic? No fair, Peking!"

Any thought of avoiding Burke was now out of the question. With one hand under her elbow, he was propelling her along toward the bus, the last of the departing crowd.

As Burke sat down beside her, bulky in his sheepskin coat, she noticed that he cast one quick, appraising glance over the bus as though checking on the welfare of the company of which he was in charge. He glanced out the window at the gray city rolling past them, and it occurred to Gillian that he could run *that* teeming entity too.

The driver was giving them a rough ride. He was either unskilled or had been shaken up in the accident more than anyone realized. He slammed on his brakes repeatedly and never took his hand from the horn.

At one point, Burke put his arm around Gillian to steady her. She trembled under his touch; her feelings were so close to the surface when it came to him. And Burke, perhaps misunderstanding her reaction, withdrew his hand quickly.

The actors and crew began shouting, "Hey, it's too early for a roller-coaster ride" and "This way to the Chinese Thunderbolt," but Burke was quiet, and although she was careful not to touch him, Gillian was piercingly aware of that long, muscular thigh next to hers, covered in slim corduroy jeans that emphasized his masculinity. There was a smoldering force between them that separated her and Burke from the laughing crowd.

Suddenly he stiffened. He was out of his seat and running down the aisle, shouting, "Get him, somebody! He's passing out."

Holding onto the metal armrest, Gillian could see the man in the first seat knock the driver aside and grab the wheel. The bus seemed to shake itself like a wounded animal; then it came to a shuddering stop.

"Open the doors!" someone yelled. "Give the guy air."

Two men in the visored caps and white armbands of the city police entered, and Gillian went forward to help with explanations. The bus driver revived, but it was obvious that he should no longer be behind the wheel. One member of the film crew offered to drive the short distance to the Forbidden City, but the police wouldn't allow it. Instead they said they would help the company to get taxis.

Pulling rank, Burke motioned to them that he was first. When a cab drove up, he adroitly separated Gillian from the crowd and put her in it, then quickly got in beside her and slammed the door. The last thing Gillian saw was the astonished look of the people still standing on the sidewalk.

"In case the cops didn't explain it to him, would you mind telling the driver we're going to the Forbidden City?" he said to her.

Gillian leaned forward to do so, but when she sat back, she found herself encircled by Burke's arms. She struggled, angry at this latest move of his, so apt to nullify her intention to cool their relationship. "Please, Burke! I thought we settled that aspect of our relationship last night."

But he held her even tighter, his strong arms hard against her breasts. "I'm just softening you up so you won't give me any trouble on the set today."

She twisted in his arms, then drew her hand back and slapped him across the right cheek. Quickly he caught both her hands and held them in a steely grip. His eyes dancing with amusement, he said, "I thought that would get you. I won't consider our relationship 'settled,' Gillian West, till you stop playing the ice maiden with me."

"Let me go, Burke, or I'll yell rape."

"He'll probably think you're saying good morning," he said offhandedly.

"You forget, I speak the language."

"Ah, in that case..." He dropped her wrists and

wrapped her in his arms again. At the same time he brought his mouth down on hers, pressing his warm, vibrant lips on her own.

After a long time, when he finally released her, she murmured weakly, "We shouldn't, Burke." But there wasn't much sincerity in her voice, and he paid no attention. He parted her lips with his tongue and trailed it across her full, moist lower lip in strokes that excited her terribly. Then, while his mouth was in hot pursuit of more kisses, his hand slid up under her jacket, gliding around her waist, the thumb brushing the full swell of her breast.

Panting a little, she tried weakly to push him away. "People don't behave like this in cabs here. The Chinese are very puritanical."

"I know that." He pointed to a sign in Chinese characters in the cab. "'Kissing Not Permitted. Punishment: Five Years of Reeducation to Eradicate Evil Impulses.' I think it's worth it, don't you?"

Yes! Gillian felt like shouting, but she didn't say a word. His lips covered hers again in a long, delicious kiss. Then they hunted for the sensitive place behind her ear. When that had been caressed, he nibbled delightfully at her delicate ear lobe. From there he ran little kisses across the nape of her neck, setting up a path of provocative sensations like a string of exploding firecrackers. His lips followed the curve of her throat, stopping at the wildly throbbing pulse point, then reaching upward for her already parted, waiting lips.

The taxi slowed, then glided to a smooth stop.

"We're here," Gillian breathed. "It's the Forbidden City."

"Tell him to go around the block a couple of times," he suggested.

"Oh, Burke! I'd be too embarrassed."

Burke shrugged. "That's all right. I think I can swing it."

As Gillian waited, half-laughing, half-embarrassed,

Burke told the driver in simple, badly pronounced, but understandable Chinese to drive for ten minutes more. Then he leaned back and slid his hands under Gillian's jacket, pulling her close to him.

"I didn't know you spoke Chinese," she said.

"I picked up a few words on the set."

He nuzzled her throat again, letting his lips trail slowly down to its base. At the same time he caressed her breasts. The feel of his strong, gentle hands gave her exquisite pleasure. She had a softness, she thought, for his every hardness.

But the second time they rounded Tien An Men Square, she pushed him away resolutely.

"This is madness, Burke. You shouldn't be late to the set. They can't start without you."

He sat back. "You're right. Today's going to be a tough one, too. So don't give me any static, please, Gillian."

All the joy she had just experienced in Burke's arms was wiped out by this flippant, condescending remark, an indication of his arrogant assumption that her efforts to keep *Siege* historically valid were just "static," to be turned on and off at his will.

"I'm being paid by Griffon Studios to be an objective, impartial observer and consultant. I'm *not* being paid to 'see things your way,' 'be on your side,' or 'not make static.'"

She could hear her voice rise, but she didn't care. Anger was a relief—anger at him, anger at Andrea, anger at their Hollywood for playing by different rules than her Haywood, and at herself for yielding to Burke again.

At Burke's command the driver brought the cab to a full stop. Outside the window lay the awesome expanse of Tien An Men Square and the vermilion walls of the Forbidden City.

Burke laid his hand on her arm. "Don't be mad, Gillian. Let's start the day friends."

Gillian didn't answer. They could be lovers or enemies—but not friends. That last, Gillian now saw, was an impossibility. There was no going back to square one and a friendly, casual working relationship. There was only this powerful, tidal attraction between them, pulling them together like earth and sea, then drawing them apart again.

chapter 5

ALTHOUGH SHE HAD seen it before, Gillian thrilled anew
to the splendor and exotic beauty of the Forbidden City—
the vast courtyards and purple-walled palaces with their
mustard-yellow tiled roofs, the upswept eaves crowned
by ceramic figures—protectors, according to Chinese
mythology, of the buildings and people within—and the
white stone terraces that held bronze tortoises and cranes,
ancient symbols of longevity. In the days of Imperial
China, smoke rising from these bronze incense burners
would announce the emperor's decree to the rows of
kneeling government officials that filled the enormous
courtyard.

This complex of palaces, temples, and ceremonial
halls, now the Palace Museum and open to all the people,
had been called the Forbidden City because, in Imperial
China, ordinary people were not allowed to come near
it. It consisted of a series of courtyards and pavilions

with poetic names: the Hall of Perfect Harmony, the Hall of Heavenly Purity, the Hall of Mental Cultivation, and—Gillian's favorite—the Hall of Three Rarities, where one of the emperors had kept three prized copybooks of calligraphy by three celebrated ancient Chinese calligraphers.

Behind the Hall of Preserving Harmony was a two-hundred-ton marble slab over which the emperor's sedan chair was carried by bearers who walked up the pair of stone staircases that flanked it. The huge stone block, which was carved with cloud and dragon designs, had been quarried far from Peking and brought to the palace in the winter by sliding it over an ice path made by pouring water onto the road and waiting for it to freeze. Wells had been sunk along the way in advance to provide water.

Inside, the palaces were filled with jade, gold, and ivory treasures—or what was left of them. The Imperial Palace had been sacked many times, beginning with the Boxer Rebellion, when wagonloads of priceless objects had been carried off by looters from the victorious Allied forces.

Now, alone in the courtyard where the climactic scene of the film was to be played, Gillian skimmed through the synopsis of the story, which she had brought along to refresh her memory.

The siege of the legations had been lifted by an Allied relief force, and the soliders and civilians of all the nations intended to mix profit with punishment. The Americans had been forbidden to join in the looting but did so anyway.

With the defeat of the Boxers, the Dowager Empress Tz'u-hsi had fled the Imperial Palace in the clothes of a Chinese peasant. The city of Peking lay wide open for looting, rape, and murder. And the Forbidden City, with its fabled treasures, was the golden object of everyone's desire.

In the film synopsis, worried about the fate of her

friend Feng Yi, lady-in-waiting to the Empress, Andrea goes to the Imperial Palace. In room after room she sees men, many of whom she has entertained at the American legation, carrying off precious silks, pictures, porcelain vases, jade carvings, gold clocks, and other treasures. Some of the court eunuchs stand watching, and she asks them if they have seen Lady Feng Yi, but they move away from her and don't answer. When she finally finds her friend, Feng Yi has hanged herself with the golden tassel of her gown, which has been half-ripped off her, an obvious sign that she has been raped.

That scene, an interior, was to be shot later in the day. At the moment technicians were still setting up the courtyard scene, in which Andrea, distraught at finding her friend's body, rushes out into the courtyard and comes upon a group of looters, loaded with booty from the palace. Her husband is among them. He boasts to her about the silks and precious furs he has taken. All her contempt for him surfaces. She coldly humiliates him in front of the others, then brazenly walks away with her lover, the lieutenant, who has come to stop the looting. When they reach the Empress's garden behind the palace, she breaks down. He urges her to run away with him, but she refuses to cause a scandal that will ruin her husband's career.

As she read the synopsis, Gillian was peripherally aware of the crowds of Chinese and foreign tourists who were jostling one another and stretching up on their toes for glimpses of the preparations going on in a sealed-off part of the courtyard. Even she was having her picture snapped.

Slowly, deliberately, she folded the sheets of paper and tapped them against her fingers. She surveyed the Chinese and American grips wheeling cameras and lighting equipment across the set. Her eyes rested on the actors standing at the food wagon, drinking coffee and eating breakfast rolls of unsweetened dough fried in oil; and on the private dressing trailers where the film's stars were, while the extras strolled about in flapping, worn sandals, their hair falling in a single pigtail down the back of their ragged shirts.

She dreaded having to tell Burke that there was something wrong with one of the scenes. Her emotions were tuned to such a fine pitch where he was concerned, she didn't think she could stand another quarrel, another sarcastic remark about his "lady historical consultant," another one of those cold looks that turned his eyes into slivers of blue ice.

But she had to. The suicide scene was completely unauthentic. No Chinese lady of high rank such as Feng Yi would expose herself half-dressed even after death. It was absolutely unthinkable.

When Burke seemed relatively unoccupied, she walked across the set to him. With that sixth sense they had for each other—"heat-seeking missiles," she thought wryly— he raised his head and watched her coming.

Even there on the set, his eyes had an intense, caressing look as they roamed over the delicate curves of her body. Her pulses thudding, she unconsciously arched her back so that her breasts lifted under the beige turtleneck and chocolate-brown wool blazer she wore.

"Everything okay, China Girl? I saw you reading the story synopsis."

She hesitated. Everything in her wanted to say yes. She didn't want to play *Two for the Seesaw* again. She just wanted to stay in the middle, perfectly balanced, where emotion wouldn't touch her and she couldn't be hurt.

Then, afraid that if she hesitated too long she would weaken, she blurted out, "The scene in which Andrea finds Feng Yi hanging there has problems."

"Like what?" His voice was sharp, his dark blue eyes wary.

"Wouldn't this high-born Chinese woman arrange her clothes so she'd be completely covered before she committed suicide? She'd know she'd be found like that and stared at by strangers."

He drew his dark brows together in a moment of thought, then spoke rapidly, decisively. "I want the audience to see at a glance what Andrea sees—that Feng Yi has been raped. She doesn't care about arranging her clothes. All she wants to do is die as quickly as possible, because she's covered with shame and can't stand it— not for a single minute."

Gillian looked unconvinced, and Burke continued with more intensity.

"Look, I don't want an academic discussion about rape. I want it seen, made visible, shockingly visible, on the screen. That's what movies are about."

Listening to his harsh, machine-gun delivery, Gillian thought, he's under terrific tension, that's why he's flaring up so fast. She was determined to remain reasonable—until he finished with a patronizing "do you understand?"

Then she hit the ceiling. "I *understand*, all right. I also understand that the test of a director's ingenuity is his ability to express something in more than just one way. You're painting yourself into a corner, Burke. *Siege* will be a hit in Times Square and maybe it will play in Peoria, but the Chinese won't buy it."

"Nevertheless," Burke growled, "the scene's staying the way it is."

They were still standing facing each other like two fighters squaring off, when Andrea emerged from her trailer, carrying a parasol and wearing the high-necked shirtwaist, fitted jacket, and long skirt of the period. Her black hair was piled high under a white, plumed hat, and her bearing was regal.

Gillian could see at a glance why Burke had wanted her for the role. She was perfect for it—the very picture of a courageous woman who dared to be different, who refused to love a man unworthy of her even though he was her husband, and who rejoiced in having a Chinese friend.

Yet it was obvious there was something radically wrong

with Andrea this morning. She kept wetting her lips nervously with her tongue, which meant she'd have to be made up again, and the gloved hand gripped the folded parasol so tightly, the outline of the knuckles showed, sharp and prominent.

"I'll talk to you later," Burke said, and walked, with his lanky stride, over to Andrea. Gillian watched as those violet eyes looked beseechingly up at him, as the full bosom heaved and one hand ran caressingly up and down his arm.

"Lady in distress," Gillian thought contemptuously, turning away. Andrea's latest off-stage act, and Burke was falling for it. Or was it an act?

As Burke kept rehearsing a piece of business in the courtyard scene with Andrea, it was obvious something was wrong. For the first time since Gillian had joined *Siege,* Andrea wasn't delivering the reaction Burke wanted. She kept blowing her lines or making awkward, staccato gestures. She would alternate between being strident or almost apathetic. She didn't seem able, no matter how hard Burke worked with her, to strike the right tone.

Yet he never lost patience. He told her what he wanted, showed her, and gently led her through it step by step. Finally, wearily, he shouted to the crew, "Okay, let's do it."

The familiar call of "Action! Roll 'em!" was heard. Gillian hardly dared to breathe. It was obvious Burke was at the end of his rope. He sat slumped back in the director's chair, his long legs stretched in front of him. He had pulled his cap down so it half-hid his face, though Gillian could see the line of his clenched jaw.

The scene began with the lieutenant, played by handsome, blond Trent Baylor, reminding the diplomats pawing through a trunk of priceless silks that orders had been issued forbidding Americans to loot, no matter what the other legations were doing. Andrea was then to enter after finding Feng Yi's body, listen to her husband gloat over his booty, contemptuously call him "scum" and a coward, and slap him across the face.

Trent, as always, was the epitome of cool, the complete professional. He went through the scene without a mistake and, Gillian knew, without having needed much rehearsing.

Andrea's performance was marginal. She seemed more nervous than angry in the scene, more hysterical than contemptuous. Gillian wondered if Burke, with his high standards, would let her go on like that.

In the middle of her tirade at her husband, he yelled "Cut!" He jumped out of his chair and strode across the set to Andrea. With a visible effort at self-control, he showed her once more how he wanted her to stand, the angry gestures she should use, and the furious, outraged tone of voice the scene called for.

The morning wore on, with take after take. Everyone was becoming increasingly tense and irritable. Finally, throwing up his hands, Burke called for a break and walked off the set.

Gillian followed the crowd to the lunch wagon but dawdled a little, watching Andrea. To her surprise, the star didn't head straight for her dressing trailer, as she usually did after a scene. Instead she stood apart from the crowd, twirling her parasol on the ground, a faint smile on her cameolike face. Andrea was waiting for someone.

Not long after, Burke came up to her, bent his head over hers, and stilled the hand on the parasol. Then, one arm familiarly around her waist, he walked the actress to her trailer. The door shut on them, and Gillian slowly moved up the lunch line, her heart dulled by a pain she tried to ignore.

She carried her styrofoam cup of hot tea to a low wall and sat in the pale April sun, fighting off the web of depression that enveloped her. Why was Burke always so tough on her and tender with Andrea? What hold could the actress possibly have on him except that of love? She might be insecure about that love—her bout of nerves and inept acting were more than likely designed to attract Burke's attention as it strayed to Gillian—but how justified was that insecurity?

Not very, Gillian decided. Oh, sure, Burke was attracted to his "lady historical consultant." But that was all he felt. A man like Burke probably lit many candles, but only one would burn with love's bright flame.

And what of her, Gillian? Was this dull ache in her heart a sign of wounded love? It couldn't be. Hurt pride was more likely. She had been more careful with her heart this time than she had been with Elliot.

A shadow darkened the cobblestones in front of her. She looked up into the affable, smiling face of Paul Rogers.

"I hope you don't mind my gate-crashing. I was on my way to my office, saw the filming going on, and couldn't resist."

"I'm delighted you came, Paul. If I had known you were interested, I would have gotten you a pass."

"I'd like that. I'm a real film buff."

Curious, Gillian asked, "How did you get past the guards?"

"Easy. I flashed my California driver's license at them. Say, if you're free, how about keeping that date to help me shop for souvenirs?"

"Can you take the time in the middle of the day?"

"Sure. My time's flexible," he assured her. "I'm a consultant, remember. So are you."

The temptation was overwhelming. The chance to escape from the tedious repetition of rehearsals and takes, from the sight of Andrea and Burke together, and from the unavoidable confrontation over the suicide scene seemed heaven-sent.

"I'd love to," she said simply. Looking around, she added, "But I should let somebody know that I'm going."

She spotted Dan Ross in the crowd around the lunch wagon. Then her glance drifted to Andrea's trailer. Burke was closing the door behind him, his face grim.

With a choice between the two, she decided on Dan. "If you'll wait here a moment," she said to Paul, "I'll tell the production assistant I'm taking off for a few hours. I'll have to be back by afternoon, though."

"So will I. Say we spend an hour on the Street of Antiques, then have lunch at the International Hotel. You'll be back on the set by early afternoon. All right?"

"Yes, fine."

"Give me fifteen minutes or so to make a few quick calls in my office. Then I'll get one of my company's chauffeured cars and pick you up here."

Gillian nodded abstractedly. Dan had disappeared while she was talking to Paul, and now Burke was striding toward her, his expression somber. Whatever had happened between him and Andrea in her trailer evidently hadn't been to his liking.

"You remember Paul Rogers," she said, waiting for the men to shake hands. "Paul and I are going to the Street of Antiques for an hour or so, Burke. You won't need me for the courtyard scene, and I'll be back before you start shooting the interior—your suicide scene," she added pointedly.

This time he gave no quick, funny answer. For a second she felt sorry for him. Deep lines furrowed his cheeks from his blade-straight nose to his mouth, and his eyes were dulled with fatigue. Well, he had Andrea to comfort him for the frustrations and anguish of film directing, she thought wryly. It was every man—or woman—for himself in this world. And this woman wanted—needed—to get away.

"Go ahead," he said wearily, passing his long brown hand across his forehead. "Take Keng. Just make sure you're back for the afternoon's shooting."

"I have a car and driver," Paul said, bristling a little.

Burke paid no attention to him. His sapphire-blue eyes held Gillian's. The sardonic light was back in them.

"Take Keng," he repeated. Then, with a quirk of his

eyebrow, he added, "As chaperone."

He turned on his heel and marched back across the set. And to think only seconds earlier she had felt sorry for him.

Gillian shrugged. "We might as well go with Keng. He's an excellent driver and knows Peking well."

Paul smiled good-naturedly. "That's more than I can say for our drivers. I think they were all born in Brooklyn."

"Then I'll pick *you* up in fifteen minutes."

Paul nodded. "In front of the hotel."

Gillian walked across the street to where the company's cars were parked. She found Keng's Shanghai and got in.

"The International Hotel, please, Keng, and then Liu Li Chang."

Keng flashed her a big smile. She knew he loved having her in his car because she spoke Chinese, enabling her to help him overcome his struggles with the English language.

He often brought his questions to her. Today he had no sooner swung out from the curb than he looked at her in the rearview mirror and said, "English teacher on radio say *e* in love not pronounced. Is 'quiet *e*,' like in move and food."

Gillian repressed a giggle. "Move has a silent *e*, but food does not. There is no *e* in food. It's spelled f-o-o-d. No *e*."

Keng shook his head. "English very hard language to learn."

"English *is* a very hard language to learn," Gillian corrected.

"You think so too?"

Gillian laughed outright this time, and Keng good-humoredly joined in.

When Paul got in the back of the sedan, Keng started making his way across the city to Liu Li Chang, the Street of Glazed Tiles, also known as the Street of Antiques.

"Why is it called the Street of Glazed Tiles?" Paul asked, placing his hand over hers, where it lay on the gray upholstery.

"Because there used to be glazed-tile works there. They were built in the fifteenth century to make the tiles for the new Ming palaces. In the middle of the seventeenth century, small shopkeepers, particularly booksellers, moved into the area, and it became a meeting place for scholars." He interlaced his fingers with hers while she spoke. "Then printers and antique shops followed. Later it became a marketplace for antiques, old books and scrolls, paintings, and curios of all sorts."

Paul gazed into her eyes and gave her hand a slight squeeze. "It's like old times, isn't it, Gillian?"

Not, she thought, if you were a stickler for accuracy. She had never ridden in the back of a car with Paul and held hands.

"Old friends are always comfortable," she said with a slight laugh.

"You're not the kind of woman who looks for comfort."

"No?" Her laugh deepened. "What do I look for, then?"

"Romance. Love." He reached for her, but she stopped him with one outstretched hand. "The driver," she murmured, motioning toward Keng's dark crew cut and protruding ears.

With that Paul sat back, and they chatted about people they knew at Haywood. But all the while Gillian thought, Burke wouldn't have given up so easily. He would have said, "To hell with Keng" and pulled her close to him, pressed his lips to hers, ruffled her hair, called her "China Girl."

Forcing her thoughts away from Burke, she smiled at Paul and laid her hand on his arm.

"Old times," she said. "They're the nicest."

Then Keng was parking the sedan and pointing to the place where he would wait for them.

"Grab your hour," he said graciously.

"Take your time," Gillian automatically corrected.

The narrow street was lined on both sides with shops whose dark wooden fronts leaned drunkenly against one another. On a broken sidewalk, children played ping-pong, using no net and no paddles, just a dented celluloid ball, which came flying through the air at Gillian.

She caught it and threw it back, calling out *"nee how"* at the same time.

Her ability to say hello in their language sent the children into a fit of giggles, and they cheerfully sing-songed back, *"shee-eh, shee-eh"*—"thank you"—and returned to their game.

Paul and Gillian browsed in many stores, crowded with tourists of all nationalities, looking at scrolls and snuff bottles, Chinese lanterns and lacquer boxes, stone Buddhas and *chops*—the personalized stamps in the shape of the imperial lion, pagodas, tortoises, or any kind of figurine that could be carved out of jade, onyx, marble, or soapstone. Your name was etched on the bottom in Chinese, and a pad of red ink could be purchased at the Peking Department Store.

One store was knee-deep in Americans, printing their names on pieces of paper in English so the clerks could reproduce them on the *chops* they were buying.

"Hell's bells," a man in a visored golf cap and plaid jacket said to his wife. "Put down 'Rin-Tin-Tin' and let's get out of here. Sounds Chinese, anyway."

Gillian helped Paul order a set of *chops* for a nephew. Then they separated, Paul to shop for a scroll and Gillian to look for jade earrings for her mother. Several times she had tried to find a suitable pair of earrings that wouldn't detract from her mother's small, oval face—a face so similar to her own. But so far she hadn't found what she wanted.

She had one more shop to go into, a dimly lit storefront and the most decrepit building on the street. The wood floor was full of splinters. The Buddhas behind the smeared showcases looked like Hollywood Boulevard instead of the real thing. The store was the kind where tourists drifted in, took a look around, and left.

But when Gillian explained to the serious-eyed owner what she was looking for, he brought out a case of exquisitely carved jade earrings. She had just selected the smallest, most delicate pair, when a familiar voice murmured at her elbow, "I saw the same earrings on Rodeo Drive at half the price."

Gillian turned, surprised, to see Dan Ross. "I think you're jealous because I got the only ones," she said, smiling. "You're a dog in the manger, Dan."

"More like a mangy dog. I had my hair cut in a barber shop, and he gave me the pre-Mao look." Dan ran his hand over his ragged locks.

"You look fine," Gillian said soothingly. "Are you shopping for souvenirs too?"

"Sort of," Dan said evasively. "Burke gave me time off for good behavior—about an hour. The shooting was going so slowly, anyhow, it didn't matter whether I was there or not."

Gillian wanted to hear more about what had happened after she left the set, especially what Dan thought was wrong with Andrea. But Paul came into the store just then, a long roll of paper under his arm.

"Wait till you see what I've got *here*," he said excitedly after she had introduced him to Dan. "It's a real beauty."

He unrolled the paper and revealed a black-and-white drawing of a Buddha, its face a model of dignity and serenity.

"It's a rubbing of a bas-relief carving over 2,000 years old."

Dan and Gillian dutifully admired the picture. Then Dan excused himself with, "Got an errand to do," and left.

Gillian and Paul returned to Keng's Shanghai.

* * *

Gillian had no sooner walked into the International Café than she saw them—Burke, Andrea, Robyn, Phil Grossman, and Trent—sitting around a table with drinks and food in front of them. She had known Burke liked to eat and drink with his actors. They were a team, and intimacy helped preserve that spirit.

With the sixth sense that always seemed attuned to her presence, Burke looked up at just the moment when Paul put his hand around Gillian's waist to guide her past a knot of noisy drinkers at the bar.

Granite-faced, Burke half-rose, then introduced the other people at the table. "Sit down. Join us for lunch," he invited them.

Obviously excited at the prospect of lunching with a famous Hollywood director and his stars, Paul started to say yes, but Gillian stepped in with a polite refusal. She didn't trust the mischievous gleam in Burke's eye. The coming hours on the set would be trying enough, she reasoned. And she led the way to a nearby table.

"What'd you do that for, Gillian?" Paul asked, his small, neat mouth drooping with disappointment. "I told you I'm a film buff. I would have liked to eat with them."

"I'm sorry, Paul. I just . . . well, I wanted a change of company, I guess."

A pleased, rather smug smile replaced the pout. Gillian had the sinking feeling that Paul was developing certain ideas about her. She had no intention of leading him on and didn't want to hurt him. But she saw him only as a friend and an unwitting buttress against Burke.

Glancing over at the other table, Gillian wondered amusedly just how long Paul's awe of the stars would have lasted. Trent, obviously bored, was doodling on a map of Peking spread out before him. Andrea was moodily spinning her half-empty glass with her index finger, while Robyn and Phil gazed deeply into each other's eyes. Robyn, Gillian was amazed to see, had a cup of coffee, not a drink, in front of her. Burke, on the other hand, was scowling into a tall Scotch.

"For God's sake, stop that," he snapped at Andrea. "Do you want a refill? If you can't drink it, don't play with it."

Andrea stood up. "I'm going to my hotel. Is your driver still out there?" she called across the empty intervening table to Gillian.

"Probably. He was going to buy his lunch at a street shop and eat it in the car."

"Will he understand if I tell him White Cloud?" the actress asked haughtily.

"He'd understand if you said 'mackerel sky,'" Gillian replied proudly. "I've been giving him English lessons."

"Would you mind taking a taxi instead, Andrea?" Burke intervened. "The boy at the lobby desk will get one for you. He'll also tell the driver where to go and pay him in advance. Oh, and Andrea," he added in a coaxing tone, "try to get some rest, will you? Remember, we want to do that suicide scene early in the morning."

Without answering, she left the table and strode across the lobby. Heads turned as she went by. She was wearing boots and a long, full skirt, and had draped her magnificent shoulders in a heavy fringed shawl.

"She'd make a superb Catherine the Great," Paul said admiringly. "You know, it's amazing. I looked at her pretty closely when we were introduced, but I couldn't see a single scar from that plastic surgery she had."

"Plastic surgery?" Gillian was stunned by this revelation.

"After that auto accident five years ago. Didn't you read about it? It got a lot of publicity."

"No." Gillian smiled. "I'm not the film fiend you are." All the while she was turning over in her mind this new piece of information about Andrea that no one had ever mentioned to her. "Is that why she dropped out of films?"

"Yes. I guess she was really smashed up badly. But she certainly looks wonderful now."

Gillian couldn't deny *that*.

Gillian looked across at Paul, methodically dabbing his mouth with a napkin. "Early in the morning," Burke had said. That meant they wouldn't be shooting that afternoon, and Gillian had the feeling that Paul would be more than willing to take the afternoon off and go somewhere with her. But did she want to spend the rest of the day with him, or should she go back to the hotel and catch up on her letter writing?

Trent left next, his map of Peking neatly folded and shoved in a back pocket. "Going to the Ming Tombs," he called out cheerfully to Gillian.

Then it was Robyn and Phil's turn. As Robyn passed, her arm linked in Phil's, she gave Gillian a big smile and a wink.

With Burke left all alone, she invited him to their table. He sat politely while Paul and Gillian ate their lunch, and answered Paul's questions about film making, and directing in particular. He finally told Gillian that they had to stop shooting that afternoon because of Andrea.

"I've never seen her like this," he said, shaking his head. "She's as much a pro as Trent, and now she's fluffing her lines and screwing up her body language like some rank beginner. I wish I knew what was bothering her. But maybe an afternoon's rest will do the trick. We've been pushing pretty hard."

Paul's face brightened. "Say, if you've got the afternoon off, Gillian..."

Burke interrupted, his voice bland, an impassive look on his usually intense face. "Gillian and I are going to the Great Wall."

The sheer effrontery of his statement so amazed Gillian that her only response was, "I've seen the Great Wall."

"But *I* haven't. C'mon, you'll love it even more the second time."

He was on his feet then, pulling her out of her chair,

telling Paul how sorry he was that they had to rush off like this. Gillian flushed at his high-handedness. Peripherally she caught Paul's look of bewilderment, before she jerked her arm out of Burke's grasp and hissed, "Let me go, you big bully!"

Paul was on his feet in an instant. "Let the lady go, Ferrara."

The men faced each other with the table between them. Their eyes locked in combat; their hands were fists.

"The *lady* happens to be on the company payroll. I need her services as an interpreter this afternoon." He turned to Gillian. "Let's go," he said curtly.

Apologetically, she said goodbye to Paul, and he answered in a quiet, tightly controlled voice, "I'll call you, Gillian."

Burke's hand was on her arm again. His mouth had settled into a thin, straight line. And the expression on his face as his navy blue eyes raked over Paul was a storm warning.

chapter 6

GILLIAN WAS STILL seething as, his hand under her elbow, Burke steered her toward Keng's gray sedan. But part of her anger, she knew, was directed against herself. For she had to admit it secretly thrilled her to know Burke wanted her company so badly.

Still, he had to be taught a lesson. She wasn't his personal possession, a rag doll to be swept up and carried off when he wanted. So, seating herself as far away from him on the gray plush seat as possible, she recited in a monotone, "The Great Wall of China is four thousand miles long and was started in the third century to protect the country against northern invaders. The part we're about to see is thirty feet high and twenty-five feet thick. The entire wall has twenty-five thousand watch towers. Moreover, the Great Wall was the only manmade object the astronauts could see from the moon."

"I'm not interested," Burke said, interrupting her.

"You're not *interested!*" she said in mock annoyance. "Then why are we going there? I mean, why did you insult my escort and practically kidnap me if you didn't want to see it?"

"So we can be alone," he answered honestly, pinning her with his eyes. "And a car with a driver who's learning only ten English words a day seemed like the best bet."

Her heart quickened, and her blood seemed to race through her veins. She could feel the hot color mount to her cheeks. But, forcing herself to sound cool, she said, "Don't kid yourself. Keng knows all about the silent *e* in love and food."

"So the *e* in food is silent." One eyebrow arched skeptically. "I never knew that."

Gillian looked out the window and smiled. The fields along this northern road were still brown with their winter fallow, and the mountains that rose in folds on the horizon were brown too. But the trees had started to bud—a green so faint as to look chartreuse against the shiny black branches. And Gillian felt spring-green inside, too. Elliot had been the winter of her life, and the six months since her divorce had not been much better. Now she felt totally, buoyantly alive. There was a man in the center of her life—an exciting, exasperating, unpredictable man, a man who fired her senses and dominated her thoughts, a man she suddenly realized she'd be a fool to keep at arm's length.

"Just how friendly were you and that guy Paul?" Burke asked, his sea-blue eyes stern.

"He was really just a close acquaintance," she answered demurely, teasing his jealousy a little.

"Do you get paid extra for being difficult or is it just part of the job?" There was a dangerous glint in his eyes.

"Accuracy and precision are important," she replied in defense.

"Not always. How can you have an accurate emotion? Can you say 'I love you precisely'?"

She started to answer, but he stopped her, his lips pressed hard against hers, his breath warm in her mouth. Enveloped in his arms, she filled her nostrils with the pungent, male smell of him.

His hands came up then and cupped her face. His lips seized hers thirstily again and again. His kisses went deep, to the very core of her being, stirring her to a strange kind of lassitude. She met him halfway, locking her hands behind his neck and pulling his lips down to hers.

Then he touched her gently, one strong hand caressing the clean line of her jaw, drifting down the white column of her throat, and pausing where the softness of her breast began. She arched her back, lifting her breasts for his kiss, but this was hardly the place, and slowly, reluctantly, she drew herself out of his arms.

He raised a quizzical eyebrow and fixed her with a long, searching look. "Did you and this guy Rogers have a date to meet today? Is that why you went storming off the set?"

"I didn't go 'storming off the set' and I don't have to use subterfuge to meet my friends."

As much as it thrilled her to have Burke jealous of Paul, she didn't want to be *possessed*—not by him or any man. Love had to be free or it couldn't exist. Then her thinking was brought up short. Burke had never said he loved her. And she hoped she didn't love him. She had been burned once; she was wary now. Love could be a bright flame—or, as with Elliot, a cold, gutted candle.

"You're right," he said lightly. "I just hope the next time the studio sends me a historical consultant she has flat feet and dentures. Maybe that way she'll stay on the job."

"Oh, poor you!" Gillian teased. "You know, I think you're becoming paranoid."

He laughed shortly. "Most directors are."

"What led you to become a director?" she asked, hoping to learn more about the unpredictable man seated beside her.

"*Led* is the right word. I was hooked after my first war movie. I didn't want to describe war, I wanted people to feel what it was like. I wanted them to suffer by watching, because until you get enough people to feel what wars are really like, you'll always have them. In my opinion, the best way to stop them is through films."

"I don't think I ever saw any of your war movies."

"They weren't that great—though they were the best I could do at the time. They told the story I wanted, but a little more crudely than I would tell it today." He grinned. "The critics say my style is still evolving. Could be. I wouldn't know."

The grin faded. His dark lashes half-hid his blue eyes as his gaze traveled slowly down her body, lingering on the curve of her breasts and long, silky legs. She gasped imperceptibly and turned away, afraid to let him see the excitement building inside her.

Sliding his hand completely under her hair, he turned her head toward him. She could hear his breathing, quick and irregular, as he brought his mouth down to hers. His demanding lips pressed hers; his tongue probed the warm recesses of her mouth.

She moaned softly against his lips. In a kind of frenzy he pulled her slim body into his own masculine contours. Her arms went around him, and she felt his muscles grow taut under her hands.

He brushed his lips across her face, caressing and nibbling and licking gently. His hand, hot and masterful, reached inside her sweater and fondled her full breasts. Gillian felt the tips harden under his deft fingers. Then, with every nerve aroused and quivering, she pushed him gently but firmly away.

"Remember Keng," she breathed.

"To hell with Keng." His voice was hoarse, and he reached for her again.

Gillian smiled. She *knew* he'd say that.

Then, looking out the window, she saw, directly ahead of them, the great stone serpent, twisting its way down the deep valleys and up the steep mountainsides of the brown terrain.

"There it is," she said, her voice soft with awe. "The Great Wall."

After a long look, he said, "My God, what a sight. Stupendous!" He turned to her with a grin. "What d'ya say we skip the Wall and go to a cheap hotel instead?"

Gillian shook her head, her brown eyes alive with laughter. "Wrong country. The closest thing to a cheap hotel here is a Mongolian yurt."

"We could make it paradise."

Laughing, they got out of the car. Gillian avoided looking at Keng. From the smile on his face, she guessed he had been stealing a peek in the rearview mirror. Next English discussion: "How Round-Eyes Make Love."

The Great Wall was swarming with tourists, including Chinese. Round-faced, red-cheeked toddlers barely able to waddle in the quilted clothes put on them for protection against the wind sweeping down from the Mongolian steppes trudged along the paved incline with young parents. A troop of schoolchildren wearing the red neckerchief of the Young Pioneers stopped in one of the stone towers for a lecture by their leader.

Gillian too stood on one of the towers, the wind whistling around her ears, and imagined what it was like when the armies of long ago fought on the Wall. There would be a singing of arrows in the cold frosty air, and the clang of swords striking one another. Bodies would tumble from the high wall and lie on the hard brown earth for ravens to pick at.

She walked to the top with Burke and stood looking out across the bleak brown landscape of valleys and hills.

"Looks like the end of the world," Burke said.

Gillian looked at him. His hawklike profile and keen eyes belonged in this landscape. His hard, taut body would have been at home on the back of a wild Mongolian pony.

"What are you thinking, China Girl?"

"That you look like a blue-eyed Genghis Kahn."

He laughed. "As if being Irish and Italian weren't enough. Actually, Genghis would have fit very well into my old neighborhood. He would have made gang leader in no time. I can just see him, leather jacket and all."

"Sheepskin jacket," Gillian corrected.

"You know what the great Khan did to women who contradicted?" Burke challenged.

"Threw them over the Wall?" Gillian asked brightly.

"I'll show you." With that, he took her in his arms and kissed her masterfully on a windswept tower of the Great Wall of China.

When he finally released her, he said reluctantly, "We'd better get back and see what's doing in that intriguing movie company of mine. I mean that two ways. Robyn and Andrea are constantly at loggerheads. They have been since we started, but it's getting worse. Maybe that's what's bothering our star."

They left the Wall, with its little cluster of souvenir shops and a single camel for tourists to ride on.

"That's funny," Burke said. "One camel. Where did they get one camel? And why only one? You'd expect half a dozen, at least." He turned around and looked at the Great Wall again. "Man, what Disneyland could do with this."

"Please, spare me!" Gillian protested, laughing.

He started to kiss her on the way back to Peking, but she pushed him away. "No, Keng will never keep his eyes on the road if we start that again."

"I don't care about Keng. I care about us—you and me." Burke was adamant. "You know I want you, and I think you feel the same about me. So why do you hold me off all the time?"

The pang she felt at these words, which expressed so well how he saw their relationship—as no more than mutual physical attraction—opened her up to herself like lightning splitting a tree. She was falling for Burke Ferrara. She thought she had protected herself against love, but it had crept up on her like the incoming sea, and now she was being swept away, with no rock to cling to but her pride.

So she answered tartly, "I suppose because I'm not some stage-struck little zombie just waiting for the chance to jump into bed with Burke Ferrara, the famous director."

She saw him wince as though struck by a physical blow. Then he recovered. With a lift of one black sardonic eyebrow, he said, "Do you think those are the only kind of women I can get, lady historical consultant?"

She hated him when he called her that. She knew exactly what he meant to convey by the term. Some prissy, overly refined, inhibited pedant with all the emotional capacity of a cucumber.

"Oh, there's always Andrea, if you're looking for an exception," she snipped, unable to stop herself. "Although she did need help for a comeback, didn't she, after her accident."

"What do you know about the accident?" His eyes had gone sea-cold now. His voice was sharp. If she hadn't known him so well, she might have been frightened of him.

As it was, she answered calmly, "Nothing. I just heard there was one."

Burke grunted as if satisfied. "You could hardly miss hearing about it," he growled. "It was in all the papers."

She glanced at his angular profile as he stared straight ahead. His features were relaxed now. But why had he reacted so strongly when she mentioned Andrea's accident? What was he afraid she might have learned that was not common knowledge?

They rode the rest of the way in silence. God knows what Keng thought they were doing there in the back seat, Gillian said to herself as they got out of the car in front of the hotel and the chauffeur said, smiling, "Love has silent *e*. I will remember that."

If you missed dinner at the White Cloud, you were out of luck, because no other food was served at the hotel. Therefore the cast and crew of *Siege* were always sure to arrive on time and would arrange themselves at the round tables for eight placed against the right wall of the huge dining room.

Gillian entered, and hesitated in the doorway. If she accepted Dan's wildly waved invitation to join him at an empty table, she stood a good chance of sitting with Burke, since he and Dan often sat together. On the other hand, she didn't want to hurt Dan's feelings by refusing. Nor did she want to make a big thing out of her quarrel with Burke that afternoon by obviously avoiding him. So she slipped into a chair beside Dan's and waited with him for the table to fill up.

"Burke'll be here soon," Dan said, "along with the rest of the crowd. How do you like working with this crazy bunch, Gillian?"

She threw her head back and laughed. "I think I'm getting used to it, though it seems long ago that you met me at the airport."

Dan gave her a surprisingly penetrating glance. "That's because you've changed."

"Changed?" she asked, surprised. "How so?"

He shrugged. "You're less like a schoolteacher, I guess. More like . . . like . . ." He stopped, groping for words.

"More like a woman?" A dry voice behind them said.

"Yeah, maybe that's it." Dan was only too glad to agree with his boss, but Gillian went rigid as Burke slipped into the chair next to hers.

The table filled up rapidly after that, with Robyn and Phil, Trent Baylor, and an assistant director. Only Andrea was missing, and as though by prearrangement no one took the empty chair on the other side of Burke.

Her absence created a state of tension, however. As

the fish, meat, and vegetables were passed around the table, family-style, and conversation, mostly about the progress of *Siege,* ebbed and flowed, everyone sooner or later glanced toward the door.

But Gillian refused to join in the game, Waiting for Andrea. She told herself she couldn't care less whether the actress appeared, or how she looked if she did show up for dinner. Instead she rejoiced in the sight of a smiling, happy Robyn. Obviously Phil had found the somebody he needed to cherish and protect after the tragic loss of his family, and Robyn now had someone to give her the love she needed, for the old snappish Robyn was gone. She even got along with Dan now, and amiably compared notes with him about beaches where they had both surfed or water-skiied. But supper was obviously just a stopgap for Robyn and Phil till they could be alone. They left before the meal was over, and were followed by Trent and the assistant director.

Gillian was watching Dan flash "let's go" signals to the script girl, his current interest, who was sitting at another table, when a gasp went up from the room full of diners.

Andrea stood in the doorway, costumed like a princess in the *Arabian Nights*. She had braided her black hair and let it swing over one shoulder. Her top was a gold metallic tunic. She wore wide harem pants of a black-and-gold gauzy material, and on her feet, gold slipperlike shoes. Earrings of precious white jade and gold dangled beside both cheeks, emphasizing their high-boned contours.

Walking through a barrage of oohs and aahs, the actress made her way to Burke's table. With a flash of intuition, Gillian knew what Andrea intended. She was going to regain the ground she had lost when filming had to be stopped in the middle of the day because of her. Beneath that queenly exterior, Gillian guessed, was a dirty fighter. You didn't get to the top in moviedom without knowing how to take care of yourself.

Andrea gave Dan and Gillian a significant look. Dan got up immediately, making a comment about having to see a friend. But Gillian stood firm. She might not have sorted out all her feelings about Burke yet, but she had no intention of losing him to Andrea before she did.

In one graceful movement, Andrea lowered herself into the seat next to Burke's and touched a slim white hand to the earrings.

"They're beautiful, Burke. The only thing missing was having you put them on for me, as you used to. Remember? Before we went out to parties, when I'd sit at my vanity and you'd come up behind me and put your hands on my shoulders and—"

"Glad you like the earrings, Andrea," Burke interrupted, his voice neutral, a polite smile on his face. "Do you want dinner? Gillian should be able to persuade the kitchen staff to bring out more food."

"Not really. I just came down to thank you for the earrings. I have one of my terrible tension headaches. I'm sure you remember *those!*" she added with a charming laugh.

Burke nodded, a little grimly, Gillian thought.

"You used to massage my neck and get all the tension out. I'd work better tomorrow, I'm sure, if I could relax. Perhaps later in my room . . ."

Burke stared straight ahead without answering, and Andrea turned to Gillian. "How sweet you look in that little skirt and sweater. Maybe I could manage a bowl of soup, after all. Would you mind? I don't speak Chinese."

"Not at all," Gillian said politely, but she was boiling with rage as she went into the kitchen and asked one of the waitresses to bring out the soup tureen again. She stood in the doorway and watched Andrea and Burke. His lithe brown fingers were massaging the back of Andrea's neck. When he stopped, Andrea raised her lovely face and kissed him. Then the waitress set the soup in the center of the table and proceeded to ladle it out.

As Andrea ate, she frequently smiled up at Burke. And he smiled back, his arm thrown intimately over the back of her chair, his eyes lively with interest. It was obvious this was a couple that went together, belonged together.

Gillian suddenly longed to fill her lungs with draughts of pure, cold air, to purge her senses of Andrea's cloying perfume and her heart of its misery. Her dreams of being loved by Burke were as silly and schoolgirlish as Andrea had suggested her clothes were. She wasn't the type to whom Burke would give white jade, but more likely a good book, she thought bitterly.

She didn't return to the table but left the kitchen by a rear door. A few minutes outside convinced her it was too cold to remain there without a coat. She went to her room, where she got her all-weather coat from the wardrobe and tied a bright scarf over her hair. She paused a moment in front of the mirror.

"You fool!" she said bitterly to her blurred image.

She shut the door of her room quietly behind her, then stopped, her back to the door. At the end of the hall, Andrea's door was closing too.

Vivid images of Burke massaging Andrea's lovely white neck, of their kisses, of Andrea in Burke's arms, her ripe body molded to the hard length of his, flashed through Gillian's mind. With a choking lump in her throat, her eyes smarting with unshed tears, she stumbled down the stairs and out into the blessed night air.

She met Phil and Robyn coming in. "It's cold out there, Gillian," Robyn said. "It's a good thing you have a coat. I had to come back for one. Are you going far?"

"Just to the Friendship Store," she said hurriedly. "See ya."

She hurried past them, in no mood for happy lovers now. She had mentioned the Friendship Store, the government-run store for foreigners, off the top of her head. Now, she thought she might as well go there. She had nothing better to do, and, considering the way she felt, she'd need to walk all over Peking to get rid of her frustration. But that wasn't a good idea. The streets were dimly lit and, as in any big city, there were criminals, "bad elements," the Chinese called them.

When Gillian stepped out of the lighted hotel compound and started walking along the dark street, she felt a stab of fear. The ping of bicycle bells continued as always, but because the bikes didn't have lights, sometimes there was only a silent ghostly *woosh* as one glided by. It was eerie, and when a voice addressed her suddenly out of the darkness, Gillian recoiled, afraid.

"Excuse me, but you are American?"

Gillian could have laughed out loud with relief. This was only one more of the many Chinese students trying to practice his English on a tourist. He wasn't alone, either. Amoebalike, a body of five or six Chinese youths had flowed around her, ingesting her in their midst. Another took his turn with a polite "Where are you from in the States, please?" Someone else wanted to know her occupation "or business."

And as always when a student approached a tourist for some language practice, there were Chinese who didn't know English and never would crowding around just to observe. Tourist-watching was a favorite Chinese pastime. When a group of Western tourists poured out of a bus, it was as if the circus had come to town. Shopping in the Peking Department Store became an exercise in group consensus as men, women, and children gathered around the foreign buyers to discuss their taste and wonder out loud which item they would choose. And although foreign tourists generally ate in reserved rooms in restaurants or were screened off from other diners, the Chinese somehow managed to get close enough for a good look at these strange people who used their chopsticks to drop mushrooms, noodles, and fried fish into their laps.

Gillian was tempted now to show the boys she knew Chinese, as a symbol of a round-eye's interest in their culture, but she was afraid an even bigger crowd would gather. So she continued on her way to the Friendship Store with a procession of Chinese behind her, listening closely, she was sure, to her pronunciation of those tongue-twisting Western words.

Suddenly there was a commotion behind her. A high-pitched stream of spoken Chinese reached her ears, then Burke's low, baritone growl.

"Let me through! What the hell's going on? Leave her alone! Gillian, are you all right?"

Her heart started its senseless hammering again at the sound of his voice. She closed her eyes a moment in mingled amusement and love. If she didn't stop him, Burke would be taking on a crowd of Chinese on her behalf, undoubtedly causing an international incident in the process.

"I'm fine, Burke," she called out. "These are friends—Chinese students—and . . . er . . . others."

Then his strong arm was around her waist, almost lifting her off her feet.

"Thank God!" Burke said anxiously. "When you didn't come back to the table, I went looking for you. Robyn told me you had gone to the Friendship Store, and I was worried. These streets are dark. Then, when I spotted your yellow scarf and saw you surrounded, well, I jumped to the obvious conclusion."

"It's all right, Burke. I think they understand." More than understand—they're enjoying it, Gillian thought, looking at the sea of smiles around her.

"Maybe next time we'll sell tickets," Burke growled. "C'mon, I'm not ready to star in a Chinese soap opera."

Calling out goodbyes, Gillian let Burke propel her through the crowd and back to the White Cloud Hotel. Her mind was a welter of confusing ideas. Burke certainly hadn't stayed long with Andrea, if he had even gone to her room. And he had shown he cared for her, Gillian, when he came to her supposed defense. Or was that just his usual solicitude for a member of his company? Gillian sighed. She never knew out of which motive this complex, unpredictable man was operating.

"Disappointed that I deprived you of your little shopping trip?" he asked.

"Yes. I was just dying for one of those T-shirts with PEKING printed on it," Gillian said offhandedly.

"Why'd you run off like that, anyway?"

She shrugged. "No reason. A headache, maybe. Do I have to explain?"

"I think so," he said soberly. "There's a garden on the hotel grounds. It's called the Garden of Perfect Explanations. We're going there."

"It isn't called that!" Gillian giggled, but she let him lead her to the little parklike area furnished with benches for the hotel guests. They sat down on a stone bench by a pool fringed with willows. The white moonlight was strong enough to show the sleeping carp, reddish-gold forms suspended in the dark water.

They sat side by side for a while, not speaking, till Burke said, "It was the earrings, wasn't it?"

"Yes," she answered in a low voice.

"Andrea's an emotional waif, Gillian. She needs constant reassurance that she's loved, admired, wanted. As you know, she's been blowing her scenes badly lately. I don't know why. She won't tell me. The earrings were to show her she's appreciated, that I know she's trying. They were as much a gift from the studio as from me."

When she didn't answer, he put one finger under her chin and tilted her face up to him in the moonlight.

"You don't believe me."

Her eyes showed her mistrust.

"Dan told me he met you and Rogers on the Street of Antiques. Does a man send his assistant to pick out a gift for the woman he loves?" He drew his finger across her full lower lip. "I would never have Dan pick out a gift for *you*," he said softly.

As her eyes continued to seek the truth in his, he went on, still brushing his finger against her lip, separating it a little from the upper lip, stroking its soft underside. "If you've been seeing me with her, it's only because I've been trying to find out what's bothering her. I've had nothing to do with Andrea *that* way since our divorce."

Her eyes glowed softly now. She took his fingers in hers. "You're a mind reader," she breathed. "An evil, mind-reading magician."

He released his hand from hers then and passed it slowly over her right cheek, molding her jaw with his thumb. She thrilled to the difference between the tingling stimulation of her lips and the feel of his strong hand against her delicate bones.

"It's my job to know people," he said. "People and their feelings. And I know *you*, China Girl."

His lips reached for hers in a tender kiss. His mouth lingered on her own, increasing its pressure. Sensuously he used the tip of his tongue to trace the outline of her lips. Then there was the intimate thrill of his tongue against hers.

All her senses were focused on the kiss. The world shrank to his mouth and hers and the sinewy feel of his hands as they entered her coat and warmed themselves against her full, high breasts.

It seemed like forever before he returned her to the silent Peking night, the upswept pagodalike roofs of the hotel, and the spicy smell of junipers. Yet it was too soon.

She reached up and pulled his face down to hers again. His kisses grew wilder. This time he forced her mouth open with a passionate intensity that she matched, pressing her lips against his and arching her body against him.

He rained kisses on her upturned face, then reached under the curtain of her long, taffy-colored hair to kiss her neck and her small, exquisitely shaped ears. He wrapped his hands around her, his thumbs grazing her breasts, and drew her in closer to him.

Then, abruptly, she pushed him away.

"We can't," she said breathlessly. "We can't, Burke.

The Chinese don't approve of displays of affection in public. They're very puritanical."

"Oh, I don't know. I saw a boy and girl holding hands just the other day."

"Very funny. They're safe if that's all they do."

"That pretty much sums up your attitude, doesn't it, Gillian?"

She turned to him, surprised, and met that cool, speculating glance again. "What do you mean?"

"You know, so far and no further," Burke said matter-of-factly. "Oh, I know all about the Chinese and their strict rules of conduct, but that's really an excuse, isn't it? It's a convenient barrier you can throw up every time we come within a stone's throw of intimacy."

Her mind was a maelstrom of confusing ideas. Was Burke right? Had her two years with Elliot frozen all the natural passion out of her, turned her into the ice maiden of Burke's insults?

Maybe the fault went deeper. You always chose the mate you really wanted or needed at the time. Had she wanted Elliot because she knew deep down inside that he wouldn't make demands—physical or emotional— she couldn't meet?

She didn't know. She was incapable of sorting out her feelings there by the willow pond with Burke beside her in the pale moonlight. The only anchor she had was her knowledge and her well-honed skills of analysis and reason.

"I think I said once before, Burke, I don't go in for fun and games with the boss." She tried to speak lightly, but even to her own ears she sounded cold and rejecting.

Burke went white under his tan. The bones in his face seemed to get sharper. Those lips that had given her so much pleasure were thin with repressed rage.

But all he said was, "I'll walk you back to the hotel, Gillian."

The short walk seemed endless. She recognized a finality in his anger that rendered her desolate. There was nothing she could say that he would want to hear.

She found herself hoping the room boy would be at his desk so that she and Burke would have no choice but to say good night at her door. But as they silently, grimly, passed the linen room on their floor, she could hear youthful giggling from within. China might be a puritanical country, but no one could stop the old scenario of boy meets girl.

As they continued to walk down the long corridor, she felt a surge of anger. Couldn't he tell that her so-called coldness was only her protection against too ardent a desire for him? Her soft brown eyes quickened with her anger. Her cheeks flamed under its impact.

At her door she turned and faced him—head back, lips moist and slightly parted, a mixture of desire and rage in her eyes.

He swore softly under his breath. A long, deep shudder racked his frame. He reached behind her and opened the door, and his strong hands lifted her off the floor and put her inside and then he kicked the door shut.

Pulling her roughly toward him, he kissed her with a fury that left her so breathless that she had to break away. Then his hands held her gently, and he kissed her again and again, with tantalizing, provocative sweeps of his lips against hers.

"My God, Gillian, you'll never know how I want you, desire you . . ."

His husky voice trailed off as his mouth covered hers again. His kiss plunged her into a dark, timeless cave of ecstasy. Her body flamed up to meet his. Every part of her burned with longing for him, lay open to him, had been created for him to touch and kiss and explore. She had no intimate places she didn't want him to know.

She ran her hands along his strong neck, across his shoulders, and down his sides to his lean hips. She slid them upward under his shirt and reveled in the difference in texture between his smooth skin and hard muscle and the male fuzz on his chest.

His hands cupped her face again, and his thumbs moved slowly across her cheekbones and down to the sleek line of her jaw. *Could any other hands fit her body as his did?* They outlined the straight column of her neck and the slope of her shoulders. They slipped under her sweater and up past her slim young sides. They told her by their touch how her breasts were shaped.

His hands still on her bare waist, he pulled her even closer for a luscious, lingering kiss. Then, like a blue-eyed serpent, he flicked his tongue against her ear. Burke bent lower to kiss the hollow at the base of her throat, and a warm feeling swept over her.

Slowly he lifted her sweater over her head. As his hands moved upward, she could sense how the satiny smoothness of her skin must feel to him. Now he left little love bites on her neck and shoulders and ears. Her senses flared with desire, and he pulled her closer.

When he released her bra, she could feel her full breasts push against the hard muscles of his chest. Her nostrils savored his sharp male smell, which mingled with her own sweet scent. Mingling was basic to life itself. Why should she and Burke be denied it?

Gillian became soft and pliant in his arms. She arched her back, and he bent his mouth to her ripe, upward-straining breasts. His tongue explored their rosy peaks. Then he took each nipple gently between his teeth.

Her passion rose in ever-increasing waves as their hands and mouths pleasured each other. She trembled with her need for him. She was in a territory where principles didn't operate—outlaw territory. Even if he didn't love her as she loved him, this night would be hers.

He finished undressing her, slowly and reverently. His fingertips barely grazed her skin. They trailed over sensitive places and tantalized her till she stood before him quivering in her lacy briefs.

One of his hands cupped itself around her thigh; the other went behind her knees. Smoothly he lifted her off her feet and carried her to the bed.

Then, as always, his gentleness was followed by a spurt of raw passion. His hands became rough in their need to know her body, to possess her. His kisses burned her cool skin. She thought of the torrid desert sun in the morning, when the sands are still cold.

"Gillian, my Gillian," he whispered as he buried his face in her hair.

Her passion glowed, fired by a feeling that went far beyond sex. She undressed him as tenderly as he had her. Like a benediction to their union, the moon flooded the dark room with its light.

They saw each other for the first time. His eyes caressed her as she lay naked and yielding in the white moonlight. Then his hands made the caresses come alive on her skin, and his lips whispered promises of love against her flesh.

She looked up into his dark blue eyes, then let her gaze travel down the male contours above her. She touched the hard muscles of his thighs and felt him quiver.

The same wild tumult of desire seized them both. Gillian felt the wave curl over them, sweeping them out to the primal sea where man and woman, male and female, *yang* and *yin* became one.

Only later, when she lay next to him in the bliss of passion spent and desires satisfied, did she remember with a little smile that the accompaniment to their lovemaking had been the peal of bicycle bells outside in the streets of Peking.

chapter 7

THE FOLLOWING DAY was bright and sunny. The air was warmer. And the green of the trees was definitely brighter and fuller.

Gillian surveyed the courtyard of the Forbidden City, the scene of feverish but controlled activity as the advance crew moved equipment and made final adjustments. Men in the blue shirts and tan trousers of American Marines lolled about waiting for the "Ready!" call. Civilians in shirt sleeves and oddly cut trousers, as well as pigtailed Chinese, also waited. The stars were still in their dressing trailers.

Burke was talking to Phil Grossman. Phil left him, and with a smile that made her heart sing, Burke turned to Gillian.

"We're getting ready to shoot the suicide scene. It has to be done this afternoon, because I'm not sure how long the powers that be will hold that palace room for us."

Gillian had not expected this. But her feelings regarding the suicide scene had not changed.

"You're not going to shoot that scene with Feng Yi only partially dressed!"

"I sure am," he said laconically.

"I'm sorry, but I can't be a party to it," Gillian said seriously. "As I told you before, no Chinese lady of rank would do such a thing. The scene's wrong."

"Don't worry your pretty little head about it. I'll fix it up somehow."

As always, his condescension made her furious. "Well, you can fix it up without me. I'm splitting."

His eyes widened in fake shock. "I guess that leaves us without anyone to say how the actors' boot laces should be tied or whether the girls wave their hankies or blow their noses in them. Gee, I wonder how we'll manage."

"Just let me know when you get the award you deserve—'Best Director of Previous Years.'"

She turned abruptly on her heel and strode off across the set, head high, cheeks flaming. She seethed with anger. To have her work, so conscientious and so accurate, she knew, ridiculed and made light of infuriated her. All last night's joy was wiped out. Burke had become the arrogant, know-it-all Hollywood director again. What was more, she didn't think she could bear to stand around and watch the filming of a scene she knew was historically invalid.

When she reached the street she stopped, irresolute. All she had wanted was to put as much distance as she could between herself and Burke. Now she wondered what to do next.

She could go to the Hundred Goods Emporium, a gloomy, poorly lit three-story affair, Peking's largest store. But there was nothing she wanted to buy, and just looking at candy, cigarettes, liquor, transistor radios, shampoos and face creams, silks, and rubber-soled canvas sandals held no allure.

Nor did the local bookstore or the narrow old shopping street. She wanted to get out of the city, and when a Number 332 bus came along, she impulsively got on and paid the few *yuan* required.

The bus went to the Summer Palace, and she decided that would be an ideal place to spend the day. She only wished she had something to read to divert attention from herself. Polite as the Chinese were, these passengers couldn't take their eyes from the Westerner who was riding a city bus with them. In her brown tweed jacket and gold corduroy skirt, she felt exotic, a rare bloom in that sea of blue and gray trouser suits.

Finally the bus arrived. As Gillian passed through the red-painted gate that framed the entrance to the Summer Palace, she thought, not for the first time, how much that lovely conglomeration of pavilions, parks, and lake symbolized China's past.

It had been sacked by Anglo-French troops and burned to the ground in 1860 after the Imperial Court refused permission to European envoys to enter Peking. Thirty years later the Empress Tz'u-hsi appropriated money budgeted for creating a modern Chinese navy to rebuild her beloved Summer Palace, complete with an artificial lake. The only boat built was a two-story marble pavilion in the shape of a Mississippi paddle steamer. In 1900 this palace was looted of its priceless treasures by the troops of all the powers that rescued the foreign legations from the Boxers. Thus was the Empress punished for having foolishly supported the Boxers.

Today the gardens of the Summer Palace were filled with throngs of schoolchildren, families, and soldiers sightseeing, wearing their baggy green uniforms, the only signs of rank being four pockets for officers, and two for enlisted men. Students sketched the white blossoms of the flowering plum trees. Tourists and Chinese alike crowded onto the gorgeous marble boat. And strollers crossed the seventeen-arch bridge that rose over the misty waters of Kunming Lake to link a manmade island to the shore.

The lake and the sky were one in a single shade of gray, like a Chinese brush painting. Rowboats on the lake were the black lines of pen-and-ink calligraphy.

Gillian strolled through the Long Corridor, a walkway covered by a roof whose interior beams were painted with historical scenes and landscapes. Then she left it and walked at random, pausing to smile at a chubby-cheeked child with big, black-cherry eyes having his picture taken in the lap of a mythical bronze beast—the imperial lion. Moving on, she examined with interest the *kui long zi,* the glazed ceramic gargoyles on the upswept eaves of the pavilions, then joined the crowd watching an American couple pose for snapshots, dressed in the rented embroidered robes of a Manchu emperor and empress.

But there was no one to talk to, no one to listen to her comments on what she saw, no one to whom to say, "Look at that!" And she didn't want just anybody walking beside her. She missed Burke. The pavilions and the flowering plum trees weren't beautiful unless he saw them with her. Nothing was amusing without him.

Moreover, Gillian had begun to feel guilty about walking off the set that morning. Granted, Burke had been impossible, but she had been hired to do a job, not to go sightseeing at the Summer Palace.

Taking the next bus back to the Forbidden City, Gillian hoped the film crew would still be shooting.

She followed the black snaking lines of the light cables to one of the palace rooms. It had been shut off to the crowds of tourists, and a guard was posted at the entrance. Gillian showed her pass and walked in on the rehearsals of the suicide scene.

Burke was coaching Andrea on her reaction when she enters and finds her friend's body swinging from the rafter, a gold noose around her neck, her hair falling over her face, her clothes half-ripped off by her violator.

Gillian watched them. Again she saw the quick race of expressions across Burke's mobile, sensitive face and Andrea's attentiveness to him, her receptive awareness of what he wanted showing in her clear violet eyes.

The stab of jealousy in her heart made Gillian feel sick. She turned away, but in two long strides, with a shout to his assistant director to take over, Burke was at her side. From his smile, it was obvious he was in high spirits.

"Welcome back. You're just in time for the big scene. And I need you."

"What for? A punching bag?"

"Now, now," he said, chucking her under the chin, "none of that Hollywood paranoia. I think you may have been . . . not exactly right, but maybe not so wrong as I thought."

"You don't say. And exactly how does that work out in nondiplomatic language?"

"Confucius say, 'One picture worth a thousand words.'" He put his hand on her arm and led her to a corner of the room where a figure dressed in a resplendent, jeweled Manchu robe with wide, flowing sleeves and wearing black slippers on tiny, doll-like feet lay on a piece of canvas. Long dark hair hid the face. Burke lifted the figure in his arms, and Gillian saw it was a dummy. He opened the robe and revealed the blue cotton garments of a peasant, disheveled and ripped in many places. Fine silk underclothes showed underneath, but no flesh.

"I think this will work," Burke said. "Lady Feng Yi hangs herself, wearing the peasant clothes in which she had disguised herself. But out of modesty she first covers herself with a Manchu robe. The force of the hanging itself opens the robe, and what has happened to her is immediately obvious—I hope. I reinforced it by writing in some additional dialogue. What do you think? Will the Chinese buy it? There's no nudity, notice. Everything's in good taste."

"It's the perfect solution. You did well, Burke."

He looked around, then pulled her behind an ornamental screen that was one of the props.

"Listen, I'm sorry about this morning," he said repentantly. "I didn't mean those remarks. I was just taking the pressure out on you."

But she hardly listened, relishing instead the feel of his hands on her sides, his thumbs flat against her ribs under her breasts. To be in his hands again felt like coming home.

"I worried about you," he continued. "Where'd you go?"

"I took a city bus to the Summer Palace," she said with no apologies.

Burke sighed deeply. "That's the trouble with having a consultant who speaks Chinese. She's too independent."

"You wouldn't get anywhere with a consultant who *didn't* speak Chinese," Gillian reminded him.

"I'm not getting anywhere with one who does."

Burke slid his hand under her hair, then across the back of her neck, tilting her head up to him. He lowered his mouth slowly to her upturned lips and covered them in a long, penetrating kiss that left her quivering with unabashed desire. Holding her like that, he kissed her again, warming her mouth anew with his breath.

When he released her, she just stood there, missing the pressure of his body against hers, her lips lifeless without his kiss. He looked down at her. Gone was the tender look with which he had kissed her. Her passivity, unusual for her, seemed to have changed him. His sea-blue eyes were those of a Viking marauder, hot with desire for a captive woman.

He seized her roughly. His hawklike, angular face

swooped down on hers. This time he covered her lips with bruising, punishing kisses that satisfied her more than they hurt.

"I'm crazy about you, Gillian," he said huskily. He buried his face in her long hair for a moment, then held her at arm's length and looked down into her eyes. "I've got to get back. Give me a minute, then *you* can come out. Not that we'll fool anybody."

Gillian didn't care if the whole world knew about her and Burke. She had been a fool to worry about Andrea. As she stepped outside the screen, her whole body glowed from the feel of his passionate, impatient hands.

She listened while Burke gave an order to a grip to bring a light forward and to have the porto-cam ready for a closeup of Andrea's face. Then he said, "Take one," and the shooting began.

Gillian knew Burke had the reputation of being a quick director, generally getting his scenes in three or four takes, the result of careful preparation beforehand. But nothing prepared her for the finished, stagelike quality of Andrea's acting. All eyes were riveted on her, and breathing seemed to stop as she walked into the room in the Imperial Palace searching for her friend, saw the corpse of Feng Yi, and rushed to the body in the hope of saving the girl. When she touched her, the robe fell off, revealing the torn clothes. The actress's beautiful face became a window for the harrowing emotions she felt. It was obvious that Andrea was living the part— almost too much, Gillian felt. But there was nothing uncontrolled about her performance. The tension kept rising till Andrea covered her friend's body again and ran out the door like an avenging Fury.

"It's a wrap!" a jubilant Burke yelled. "Excellent! Print it!"

The smiling crew broke into spontaneous applause for Andrea. Burke went over to her and gave her a tremendous hug. And Gillian followed.

"You were terrific, Andrea. Just terrific," Gillian praised her.

"Thanks, Gillian, but Burke deserves at least half the credit. We're a team."

As Andrea smiled up at Burke, Gillian noticed how absolutely washed out both of them looked. The strain of day-long intense concentration was taking its toll.

Even so, Burke said, "Let's celebrate with a drink at the International. One take! That's practically film history."

"Count me out, darling," Andrea said. "I'm taking a car back to the White Cloud for some badly needed sleep. You drive hard, Burke."

"I have to," he said simply. "It's not just that we're on location and shooting seven days a week. It's all the unexpected problems. That's why I'm keeping everything flexible—shooting out of sequence and moving around from one set to another when necessary."

"Well, if you feel like a *restful* drink, Burke, you know my room number," Andrea said.

"For now, I think I'll make it the International."

As Andrea walked away, Burke said, "How about it, Gillian? Think you can stand the Café of Broken Dreams again?"

Gillian nodded, and they walked across the now-nearly deserted set.

"When all this is over," Burke said wistfully, "I'm going to take a China holiday. But I wouldn't want to do it alone." He glanced meaningfully at Gillian.

"There are guides," she answered mischievously. "In fact, the government won't let you travel around without one."

"I don't think those Mao suits do a thing for a girl's figure."

Unexpectedly he stopped short in front of Andrea's trailer and tried the handle.

"It's unlocked." His eyes held hers with an unspoken,

unneeded question, and they went inside.

She heard the door close behind her and the definitive click of the lock. Then his arms swept her to him. She could feel her breasts strain against the soft flannel of his shirt. His sinewy jean-clad thighs pressed her silken ones. His warm breath was on her face as he answered the invitation of her lips with all the strength of his male fire.

"Gillian! My wonderful, adorable Gillian!"

He said her name over and over, brushing the words into her soft lips with tender, butterfly kisses. All the while he caressed her back in long, sweeping strokes that had the effect of delayed-action dynamite.

His hand moved to the smooth white column of her neck, and she tossed her head back. His mouth touched her eyelids and cheekbones and the edge of her chin. He stroked her throat with the tips of his fingers, barely grazing the skin, bringing all her senses to the surface in waves of exquisite pleasure. Then and only then did his lips find the places his fingers had aroused.

Later he drew his finger across her lips, gently stroking and brushing them, parting them so he could touch their moist pink interior. She closed her eyes against the tantalizing delight this gave her. And her lips ached for his again. When they had been teased almost beyond endurance, she pressed her body even closer against his. Her breasts heaved as she swayed against him, and Burke finally brought his mouth down on hers. In that long, hot kiss, bodies entwined, they consumed each other, generating a body heat that melted their individuality and made them one.

His hand sought the soft round globe of her breast. Cupping her breasts in both hands, he held her and kissed her again, letting his lips linger this time as though he wouldn't—couldn't—let her go.

The buttons on her ivory blouse gave quickly under his eager hands. Her front-closing bra was no obstacle.

Released, her rosy-tipped breasts peaked under his touch and reached upward for his kiss.

Ecstasy ran through her like a river of fire. She arched her creamy white breasts further, offering her nipples to his tender lips, and uttered deep moans as he ran his tongue across each one, then around them in electrifying circles of delight. His strong hands held her hips, and his breath was hot on her body as his mouth continued to explore her soft flesh.

She slipped her hands up and under his shirt. The feel of his smooth skin and hard muscles under her delicate fingers sent shivers of joy through her. She ran her hands through the thick male hair on his chest, curling strands of it around her fingers. And when he groaned, she smiled with the satisfaction of a woman who knows how to love.

Her passion rose in ever-increasing crescendos as their hands and mouths pleasured each other. Her senses flared at the pungent smell of him. Her nerve ends lay open to his touch. She trembled with her need for him.

They moved dreamily toward the couch in one long unbroken embrace. Urgently he eased her down onto it and kneeled beside her. Her heavy hair fell around her face like a shining waterfall. He ran his hands under it and down over her satiny shoulders to the soft fullness of her breasts. Then he took one in turn in his hand, cupping it upward, bending his head to it, and taking the rosy peak in his mouth as if it were a goblet of champagne.

As his hand smoothed its way up her thigh and she shivered in anticipatory ecstasy, she heard a step outside. Terror-stricken, she hastily fastened her bra and silk blouse.

"It's nobody," Burke said, and reached for her again.

But the steps stopped outside the trailer. There was a rattle at the door and a metallic click of a key in the lock.

Burke froze, and both he and Gillian stared, transfixed, at the door. Andrea was there. Not the queenly

Andrea whom Gillian knew, but a wild-eyed, high-pitched harpy.

"So sorry! I didn't know you two had sneaked in here. I mean, how could I? But it *is* my trailer, and I did think I could come back for the medicine I forgot, without interrupting a little...what would you call it... extracurricular activity?"

Gillian reddened under this attack. She now realized that using Andrea's trailer was indefensible. She didn't know whether to apologize or let Burke handle the situation with his usual insouciance.

To her surprise, he was far from being unconcerned. Instead he apologized at length, in a soothing, placating tone. This seemed to divert Andrea's anger from Gillian to him, and the violet eyes, dark with hostility, turned away.

Finally, somewhat mollified, Andrea flounced out with a bottle of white pills in her hand, slamming the door so hard the trailer shook.

Gillian turned to Burke in amazement. "I've never seen her like that!"

Burke nodded grimly. "Andrea's not quite so bovine as she seems." He put his hand to his forehead. "I got that nick from a heavy ashtray she threw at me once after a party."

In spite of herself, Gillian was fascinated by this glimpse into the private life of the star. "Why did she do that?"

"She thought I had been paying attention to another woman."

"Had you?"

Burke grinned. "I'm only human."

Gillian turned away. Burke might be used to Andrea's outbursts, but she wasn't. And the scene had upset her. Being caught like that in Andrea's trailer made her feel cheap, and she felt a certain sympathy for Andrea too. But most of all she had been surprised by the way Burke handled the situation—almost as if Andrea were still his wife and he had been caught in a compromising situation with another woman.

"I think I need a drink," Burke said. "Let's go to the International."

That's where we probably should have gone in the first place, Gillian thought wryly.

The lobby café was as crowded as usual. Burke and Gillian stood on the fringe, looking for an empty table. A man Gillian didn't recognize came up and tapped Burke on the shoulder.

"I've got a table over here in the corner if you'd care to join me, Burke."

"Sure. Gillian, this is Henry Simpson of *This Week* magazine. Gillian West, Hank."

Hank was in his late thirties, with a mop of straw-colored hair, and the sandy eyebrows and freckles often seen on redheads.

"We're recent drinking buddies," Burke explained to Gillian.

Hank rolled his eyes. "Oh, these long, long, *long* Peking evenings with absolutely nothing to do. How's your picture going, Burke?"

Burke put his index finger to his thumb to form an *O*. "It's coming along. We might even be finished one of these days."

While Burke went to the bar for their drinks, Gillian and Hank talked about China. When Burke returned, Hank leaned forward and lowered his voice. "I think you should know that I ran into a young punk in Portland, Oregon, who says he knows Andrea Steele."

Burke raised his eyebrows. "So?"

Hank coughed, looked down into his glass, took a few sips, stared at Burke, his face grave, then said, "He's spreading a pretty ugly story."

Gillian could feel Burke tense up beside her.

"What kind of a story?" he asked dryly.

Hank hesitated again.

"Come on, out with it, man."

"You remember when Andrea went into a sort of decline after her accident—wasn't making any movies and had holed herself up on that ranch in Oregon?"

"Of course I remember. Get to the point."

"Well, this guy says he was living there too—when he was a teenager."

"Go on." Burke's voice was tight now.

"He implied there was something between them, that Andrea had lots of young boys out to the ranch, that she 'entertained' them, in a manner of speaking."

Burke's fingers curled convulsively around his glass. His face became livid.

Hank raised his arms. "Hey, don't get mad at me. I'm only telling you what this crumb said." The journalist lowered his voice. *"I* wouldn't report it, and my magazine wouldn't print a thing like that, but others would. Even a whiff of that sort of thing could kill her career and your picture. You know that."

"Yes, I know it." Burke traced an *x* in the moisture on the table. Then he looked up at Hank. "That picture of a sex-starved woman turning to young boys on some God-forsaken ranch in the wilderness just isn't true. I was a frequent visitor there. You know Andrea and I had been married some years before. Well, we simply resumed our relationship. We became lovers, to be explicit. Andrea's a very normal woman. There would have been no reason, absolutely no reason, for her to resort to such a thing."

Gillian felt her heart turn cold and stop. So it was true. In spite of what Burke told her, he and Andrea *had* been lovers after their divorce. It was ridiculous to believe that they wouldn't have been or that they weren't still. All the signs were there—their sensitivity to each other, the white jade earrings that seemed to have worked a miraculous cure on Andrea's "nerves," and Burke's apologies to her in the trailer.

And what was *her* position? Burke had once jokingly called her "his chief concubine." But every joke had a kernel of truth in it. Burke was just an older version of Dan. He was a Hollywood playboy, too old for the beaches, maybe, but a helluva guy with historical consultants.

"I read you," Hank said. "And don't worry about it. I can take care of that punk. I just thought you should know. It could be that he has blackmail in mind."

"What are you going to do?" Burke asked.

"I'll tell him what happens to people who go around libeling and slandering. Coming from me, a world-famous foreign correspondent"—Hank coughed—"that should scare him for good."

"Thanks. I really appreciate it," Burke said gratefully.

"It's a pleasure, believe me." With a "Nice meeting you, Gillian," Hank got up and left.

Burke grinned. "Maybe I won't make you a star after all, Gillian. Look at all the dirt you get thrown at you." He took her hand in his and kissed the tip of each finger. The touch of his lips was exciting, but she steeled herself against responding to it.

She had had enough of Hollywood types. For all she knew, Burke and Dan had attended the same workshops on seduction.

Abruptly Gillian pulled her hand away.

"What's wrong, Gillian? Is the ice maiden taking over again? Were we getting too close?"

She forced herself to sound cool, even languid. "Not at all. I have a date with Paul Rogers." She glanced at her watch. "And I really should be going."

chapter   8

WHEN THE DESK clerk handed Gillian the phone and she heard Paul's "Hello," she said, "This is Gillian. Is it all right if I come up?"

The way he said, "You bet!" made her pause. The lobby bar would have been a better meeting place, but the murderous look on Burke's face when she left him had made her fear a meeting between the two men.

"I'll be right up." She kept her tone neutral and cool.

As she stepped out of the elevator into the empty corridor, Gillian stopped. Her first thought after hearing Burke tell Hank Simpson he and Andrea had been lovers was to get away from him as quickly as possible, letting him know at the same time that he was not the only man in the world.

Now the full impact of his disclosure was hitting her. The result was a cold desolation in the pit of her stomach. She had lost a vital flame that had warmed and filled her with joy. She had lost love.

And she felt an overwhelming need for comfort. She wanted to be with somebody from her own familiar world. She wondered if perhaps there wasn't more validity in her running to Paul than she had at first realized. She liked him; she knew he was interested in her. What a relief it would be to find out she didn't love Burke, to get off that roller coaster of turbulent emotions and have a stable, serene relationship with a man who shared her values and attitudes.

Paul met her at the door, a broad smile creasing his neat features.

"This is an unexpected pleasure, Gillian. I had the impression you were involved with that director, Ferrara."

"I'm not involved with anybody, Paul." She stepped over the threshold and looked around. "Your room's like mine."

"The style's called Early Salvation Army, I believe. Care for a drink? I've got a bottle of Maotai I was saving for a special occasion, and this qualifies."

Gillian laughed. "No, thanks. That stuff's like white lightning. You'd have to carry me out of here."

"I think I could manage that," Paul said smoothly. "Tea, then?"

"Please."

She watched him carefully measure the green tea leaves into the porcelain cups, and thought, how precise, how methodical he is. Burke would have dumped the tea in impatiently, poured the hot boiled water over it, swearing as he spilled a few drops, and handed her the cup with a growled, "I don't know how you can drink that bilge water."

It was uncanny, but just thinking of Burke reminded her how his long, sinewy hands felt on her body, how his slim, hard-bellied torso pressed against her feminine softness. For an instant she saw his intensely alive face as he brought it down to hers for a kiss. The image of his nude body in the moonlight, the muscles rippling across his tanned back, flashed before her eyes.

The memory was like a knife twisting inside her. She forced her thoughts away from Burke and concentrated instead on Paul's blond, well-brushed hair, his regular, rather small features, set in a squarish face, his general air of good-humored competence. Here was a man she could depend on, a reasonable man, a man with whom she'd be safe.

He glanced up from the teacups and met her gaze. His pale skin took on a reddish flush. His quiet blue eyes grew tender.

"Do you enjoy your work here?" she asked, to cover the awkwardness of the moment.

"Very much." He smiled. "There's no commuting problem. My office is on this floor. Since this is considered a business floor, I also have complete privacy."

She ignored the implications of that remark and asked, "How long do you expect to be in Peking?"

"As long as I want." His eyes held hers. "I could go back to the States any time...if there was something there for me."

Gillian turned her head aside. She had no intention of encouraging Paul when she didn't know her own feelings.

"How about you? How long will you be in Peking?"

She shrugged. "Till the picture's finished, or at least the part that's being shot here."

"You sound as though you'll be glad to get back to Haywood." His tone was questioning. "I suppose the thrill's worn off. That's to say, the thrill of consorting with film stars and a famous director."

Definitely, Gillian thought. The thrill of consorting with a famous director had definitely worn off.

Paul leaned forward in the dingy armchair with the lace antimacassar that matched hers. He took her hand in his. "I can always get a teaching job at Haywood again." He grinned. "Maybe old Elliot will have left by then, gone on to bigger and better things."

Paul was nicer, more outgoing, better-humored than Elliot had ever been. But suddenly Gillian knew that a life with Paul would be one lit by starshine, a remote, cold glow that would leave her heart untouched. *Life with Paul would be like . . . a replay of her marriage with Elliot.*

She thought of Burke, and that hard, impossibly large lump came into her throat again. But it wasn't in her to cold-bloodedly use Paul to assuage the pain Burke had inflicted or to fill the empty place in her heart. She wasn't ready for another man—not yet, anyway, and, judging from how she felt, maybe never. So with a gentle smile, she pressed Paul's hand in a gesture of friendship and farewell.

But Paul misinterpreted the gesture. Surprised, she found herself being pulled out of the armchair and into his arms. His face close to hers had a quieter look than Burke's, and his lips were gentler though his arms felt just as strong.

Shocked into yielding to her need for comfort, for a balm to the wound Burke had dealt her, and even for love, Gillian returned Paul's kiss. She wound her arms around his neck and pulled his head down to hers.

Eyes closed, without intending to, she found herself pretending the lips pressed to hers were Burke's, and that the arms that clasped her were the ones she had laid in on a moonlit night.

Then, horrified by the realization of what she was doing, she put her hands on Paul's shoulders and pushed herself away from him.

They stood looking at each other a moment, Paul's eyes questioning, hers slightly ashamed.

"I'm not the one, am I, Gillian?" he finally said, with a faint, understanding smile.

She shook her head dumbly. "It would be better if you were." Her eyes sought his, honestly. "I'm sorry, Paul. I didn't intend to lead you on."

This time his smile was warm and generous. "I didn't think you were. Is it that director, Ferrara?"

"It isn't *anybody* now." Her wry tone changed to a brisk cheerfulness. "I'd better be going."

"I'll see you down to the lobby. I want to pick up some film in the little gift shop."

The trip down in the elevator was filled with small talk about Haywood again. If she had shaken Paul's equilibrium, it wasn't noticeable. To feel thwarted passion simply wasn't Paul's style.

As they stepped out of the elevator, Gillian found herself looking right into the smoldering blue eyes of Burke Ferrara. Hands in his pockets, his back against one of the pillars, he was watching the elevator.

Gillian felt her heart turn over with the thrill of seeing him and knowing he had been waiting for her, and with the fear of what he might do. Even so, as they said goodbye, she reached up and kissed Paul. She knew that Paul would construe her act correctly, as a farewell to an old friend. She was also dimly aware that the kiss could appear as public acknowledgment of a lover by the woman he had made happy during an afternoon spent together. But she didn't care.

With quick, little steps she left the hotel, hoping to catch a city bus to the White Cloud. But as she strode purposefully down the street, her arm was suddenly seized. She looked up into Burke's stormy face. She tried to shake his hand off, but he held her arm in a steel-tight grip.

"Let me go," she hissed under her breath so as not to attract attention from the crowds of Chinese passing by.

"You're coming with me."

"No!" she protested.

But her desire meant nothing, and he propelled her along the street, obviously confident that she wouldn't make a scene.

When they got to Keng's car, Burke opened the door

with one hand and held onto Gillian with the other. He gave her a slight push, and she fell backward onto the seat.

"The White Cloud," Burke yelled to the driver. He reached out a long arm and slammed shut the glass divider. Then he put both hands on Gillian's shoulders, holding her with just enough force so that she couldn't move, but not so much as to hurt her.

Sprawled like that on the back seat, her skirt up and Burke leaning over her, she felt a surge of conflicting, overpowering emotions—a searing anger mixed with humiliation, and that terrible desire for him that was a warm weakness in her loins.

"All right, tell me," he said roughly. "What were you doing with that guy?"

"That is none of your business." She spaced the words out emphatically. "I am a free agent. Let go of me and leave me alone." She struggled and tried to kick him. But he seized a silky thigh and pinned her legs together with one hand while he held her down with the other.

"No," he said firmly. "I have to know what's between you two."

He shook her shoulder a little. His hand moved farther up her thigh. Involuntarily her legs parted.

Looking up into his angry, handsome face, all she could think was, kiss me, touch me, hold me in your arms. I'll be your chief concubine—anything. The force of her longing for him was tearing at her, hollowing her out so she was nothing more than an aching void.

"Paul and I aren't lovers. I only made it seem that way because..." She stopped. She didn't want to tell him she was jealous of Andrea. She didn't want him to know what she had just rediscovered, more surely than before. *She loved him.* The realization unmoored her from her past life, her own ego, her career. All she wanted was him. What she felt was more than sexual, but it needed sex to be complete. And she desired him so, her body hurt with the longing.

Still holding her, looking down into her face, he said quietly, "Because I told Hank Simpson Andrea and I had been lovers, when I told you we hadn't been. Right?"

Her eyes gave her answer.

"Well, it isn't true. I'm surprised you didn't realize I said that only to save Andrea's reputation."

She accepted his rebuke silently. But how could she explain that it wasn't just his statement to the journalist, but everything: his placating attitude toward Andrea in the trailer, his unusual consideration of her—always putting her first? Or was she unduly suspicious? she wondered. Had life with Elliot made her wary of all men?

But as she raised her face to his again, all her doubts were swept away in a wave of love for him. Her full lower lip pouted a little. Her brown eyes became soft and yielding.

"Gillian!" he breathed, and lowered his lean body over hers. A long erotic shudder passed through her as his hips and flat hard stomach pressed against her softness.

He seized her mouth with his, thrusting deep with his tongue, seeking hers. When he took his lips away, it was only to give her tender love bites at the corners of her mouth and the moist center of her lower lip.

Her hands swept over the smooth muscles of his back. She reveled in the feel of his broad shoulders, his small, masculine hips, the athletic slimness of his flanks. All the while she could feel his sinewy thighs against hers and his mouth moving hotly across her face and neck.

She threw her head back and arched upward against him. Under her jacket his hands encircled the soft mounds of her breasts, and his lips returned to hers. He brushed them delicately, back and forth, setting up electric arcs of joy. Then he nuzzled her pink, shell-like ear, finally drawing it gently between his teeth. His hands caressed the swell of her breasts till their tips pushed against the silk fabric of her blouse. She felt her whole body straining to meet his. She wanted more than his hands and mouth could give her. She knew he too was reaching the limits of his self-control.

Then Keng started to cough. A series of short, rapid barking sounds reached them from the front seat.

"Tell him to cut out the cigarettes," Burke murmured against her lips.

In spite of the longing in her loins that still made her tremble, Gillian laughed, a low, throaty sound that aroused Burke, when she didn't want it to.

He held her closer and whispered, "Gillian, my beautiful . . ."

She didn't let him finish. "We're getting close to the hotel, Burke. That's what Keng was trying to tell us."

They both sat up. Gillian pulled at her skirt and jacket. While she patted her hair into place, she inspected Burke.

"You look like a prom-night Romeo. Here, let me straighten your collar."

When she finished, she trailed the tips of her fingers lightly down his neck. Quickly he seized her and kissed her.

"Now I'll have to fix us up all over again," she complained as he released her.

"A woman's work is never done."

His grin was wicked. And Keng smiled at them in a way Gillian preferred not to analyze.

They had passed the point of no return. They both knew it. They felt it in the way they looked sideways at each other and were careful not to touch. Gillian's emotions were in a state of turmoil. The feeling was heady, but uncomfortable too. She had to come down from that high level of excitement. More than anything, she wanted a spell of normality, a relaxation of the tension of unrelieved desire.

Burke must have felt the same need. As they stood in the lobby, each feeling uncertain, he said abruptly, "I can't face another meal in that dining room. Why don't we go to one of the new hotels and see how the other half lives? Wouldn't you like to eat a meal that's not Chinese, and dance and wear something seductive?"

Gillian looked down at her clothes and said demurely, "I thought *this* was seductive."

Burke grinned. "You'd be seductive in a gunnysack— and a lot safer, too."

Gillian glanced at her watch. "What time?"

"Eight?"

She nodded.

"I'll knock at your door," he said. "We'll paint Peking red."

On her way to her room Gillian considered having her hair done in the hotel beauty salon. She had never had her hair styled in China, and it was tempting. If she didn't like it, she reflected, she could always rewash it and use her own traveling blow-dryer and curling iron.

Reversing her direction, she took the elevator to the basement. The place wasn't busy, and the young man in charge agreed to take her right away. He led her to an old-fashioned barber's chair and tied a plastic bib around her neck. Explaining that there had been problems with the plumbing, he asked her to sit upright, then poured warm water from a tea kettle onto her hair and lathered it into an enormous ice cream cone. After he had rinsed her hair the same way, he deftly wound it around big pink rollers, tied a hairnet on her head, and lowered a cracked plastic dryer over it.

With the time to look about her, Gillian noticed a permanent-wave machine with dangling wires like the one her mother had once described to her. One young operator was having her hair styled by another, a man, while two other employees watched, gaping in admiration as he made deep waves in her hair, creating a Thirties look, even if none of them knew it.

Gillian's dryer had only one setting—too hot—and in no time her hair was dry. Her operator smoothed some white cream on it to make it shine and combed it out. Smiling proudly, he held a mirror up for her. A mass of golden-brown curls crowned her head, with a few wispy bangs falling seductively over her forehead. Her ears were exposed, and as she turned the mirror from side to side, she visualized how her dangling gold earrings would look.

Smiling to herself at her good luck in having gotten that operator and not the other, she paid him the few *yuan* he asked for and complimented him on his skill. Tipping was not allowed in China, so she made up for it in lavish but sincere praise. Then she became the center of a circle of beaming, admiring faces as the other operators came into the waiting room to see her hairstyle and say good-bye.

When Gillian packed for her trip to China, she had kept in mind the simplicity of Chinese dress—baggy blue pants and a Mao jacket, hardly the height of chic. She also knew that there were practically no night spots, where she might wear something snappy. But on the off chance that she might have occasion to wear it, she had packed an outfit she had recently bought and was dying to wear—a boat-neck tunic top in narrow paired stripes, black on sepia, with an A-line skirt in wider random stripes.

Then she chose two wide gold bracelets and gold pendant earrings. Her makeup too had a burnished look—she highlighted the gold tones in her skin and used a coppery lipstick. The eye color she used for her golden-brown brows and lashes deepened the brown of her eyes to a velvety softness.

Gillian examined the completed job in the dim light in front of the streaked mirror with a slight sense of doubt. Then, casting all such negative thoughts away, she dabbed

Magie Noire on her pulse spots—the base of her throat, her wrists, ear lobes, and hairline—and considered herself ready.

For a moment she pitied Chinese women. True, she had seen a few with permanents, principally in Shanghai, and some used lipstick, but on the whole, the choice of clothing and accoutrements for Chinese women was very limited. Getting all gussied up once in a while was like shedding an old skin and putting on a new one. Maybe Eve had learned more from the serpent than where the best apples were.

Whatever doubts the thirty-watt bulbs and marginally reflecting mirror had engendered were immediately dissipated by the look on Burke's face when Gillian opened the door to him. His eyes gleamed, and he let his breath out in a long, sibilant whistle of admiration.

"You look absolutely ravishing, Gillian. I didn't know historical consultants dressed like that."

"How many historical consultants have you known?"

"Hundreds. And they all wore cotton blouses with little round collars and scratchy tweed skirts."

"Funny, I was thinking of bringing one of those outfits along."

Burke too had dressed for the occasion, in a conventional white shirt and tie and dark business suit, giving him a smoothly handsome look that made Gillian's heart beat faster.

He took her arm and led her out the door. "I've got a cab waiting. The hotel clerk told him where we want to go."

As soon as Burke shut the car door behind them, he took Gillian in his arms, brushing her hair with his lips. "You smell terrific, like a meadow full of sexy flowers. Sexy and sweet." He tilted her face up to his. One hand curved around her jawline as he brought his lips down in a kiss so light and feathery it made her shiver with longing. The flames of desire began to lick dangerously at her senses again, but this was neither the time nor place for it.

"No, Burke," she said lightly. "I spent hours working on this effect. I'm not going to have you dismantle it in just a few minutes."

He took her hand in his and ran his fingers up over her delicate wrist. "Is it okay if we hold hands?" He kissed each fingertip and let his tongue dart kisses into the valleys between. Then his lips trailed up the sensitive underside of her arm, sending shivers of delight through her.

Burke was just reaching forward to take her in his arms again, when the brightly lit hotel loomed in front of them. Gillian's eyes opened wide at the unaccustomed luxury and newness, since everything else in China was austere. The vibrant colors were almost a shock, she had become so used to gray.

"What do you think?" she asked Burke as they stood together in the modern lobby, looking around.

"It's a nice place to visit, but I wouldn't want to live here."

"I know what you mean. It lacks the *je ne sais quoi*, that indefinable atmosphere of the White Cloud."

"*Gray* Cloud! What China couldn't do with a hundred million gallons of bleach."

"I don't know, I rather like that telltale gray. Just think what the country would look like if all those white uniforms were really white."

"Like a surgical ward, I know. Well, listen, they've got Western as well as Chinese food here. Which will it be? The thousand-flower soup or split pea?"

"We probably should treat ourselves to a Western meal . . ." Her voice hung in the air, doubtful, denying.

"But you're addicted to Chinese food, and so am I. Let's please ourselves and go to their traditional restaurant. We can tell everybody we went to the other one and had steak."

All the emphasis in Peking restaurants was on food,

not decoration, so Gillian appreciated the tasteful decor of the hotel restaurant and the quiet induced by rugs and thick draperies. There was no clattering of dishes by harried, overworked waitresses, no raised voices. Everything was calm, luxurious, and beautiful. Gillian gave herself over completely to this ambience, feeling her nerves relax as if she were in a warm bath.

The restaurant had a Western-style wine list, and Burke ordered a French aperitif, a Raphaël, for both of them. They sipped it slowly and, sitting side by side, bent their heads over the menu.

"Would you care to explain what Crossing-the-Bridge Noodles are, my love?" Burke asked.

Gillian laughed. "There's a story that goes with them."

"I figured as much. Go ahead."

"They're called that because in the days of the Imperial Court the noodles were dropped in a pot of boiling water as the cooks crossed the bridge before the Imperial City. By the time the pot was put on the emperor's table, the noodles were all cooked."

"And if you cross your bridges before you come to them, you're left with a lot of uncooked noodles on your hands."

"Right," Gillian drawled. "How would you like some Three-way Nonstick? They're made with eggs and don't stick to the spoon, chopsticks, or teeth. What do you think of that?" She placed her finger on the name printed in the menu.

Propping up the huge menu, he brought her finger to his mouth and kissed it. Then he playfully nibbled at it.

"I'd rather eat this. You know, come to think of it, this menu is big enough for us to do all sorts of things behind."

A waiter appeared at their table just then and asked if they were ready to order. Burke asked him to return in a few minutes.

"See, he heard what you said about the menu," Gillian said.

"I don't care. I'm reckless with love and Crossing-the-Road Chicken Soup and Three-way Nonstick. What else have they got on that menu?"

"Do you want the full dinner, or banquet, as they call it?"

"I didn't come here for a chicken sandwich."

They began their meal with a plate of cold hors d'oeuvres arranged in the shape of a butterfly. Then came Fragrant Crisp Duck, Prawn Slices in Red Sauce, Four Vegetable Delicacies, the Three Whites: Fish, Chicken, and Bamboo-Shoot Tips, and, finally, Floating Flower Soup.

"They have desserts," Gillian volunteered when they had finished. "Would you like one?"

"You must be kidding. They're going to have to rickshaw me to the door. But why do they serve the soup at the end?"

"They always do that. Haven't you noticed? Soup aids digestion. Therefore it logically belongs at the end of the meal."

"That makes sense." He lifted the half-empty bottle of Dom Perignon out of its silver bucket by the table. Their waiter came over immediately to pour the pale bubbly champagne. "You're not going to spoil this stuff by mixing it with tea, are you?" Burke asked Gillian.

"I think you want me drunk so you can seduce me."

"You're damn right."

"No tea," Gillian said to the waiter.

They drank the champagne slowly, looking into each other's eyes above the rims of their glasses. Gillian didn't think once of Andrea or Elliot or Paul. She didn't really care whether *Siege* was historically accurate or not.

Unable to touch or kiss in this public place, they made love with their eyes, and their desire became keener from denial.

They fell into each other's arms in the taxi on the return trip. Their kisses were hungry now. Burke's mouth devoured her, ravishing her lips and cheeks. And Gillian responded, seeking his lips, receiving his tongue eagerly in her warm mouth, reaching out to him.

He slipped the boat-neck top off her shoulder and trailed his lips over her soft, silky skin. The soft swell of her breast pushed against his roving hand, molding itself under his firm fingers. His hand explored her round hip and the long sweep of her thigh.

She moaned with the aching desire inside her. Then she caught a glimpse of the dark, stern face of the driver in the mirror. This was China, and a taxicab.

Gillian pushed Burke away. "No, Burke, not here," she whispered.

He straightened reluctantly and took a deep breath. "Somewhere in this country there's got to be a place for us, and I'm going to find it."

Then they were at the hotel. All the way up in the slow-moving elevator, Gillian didn't know whether to hope the room boy would be at his desk or not. She wanted Burke with every fiber of her being. Even here in the elevator, they had to touch. His hand rested intimately on her hip, and all her senses were concentrated excitingly on that spot.

But Burke had never said seriously that he loved her, she thought sadly. In fact, she still wasn't completely convinced he wasn't emotionally linked to Andrea. It would be better if the room boy *were* on duty, thereby putting an obstacle, even if only a slight one, in their way.

When they stepped out of the elevator, her heart was beating fast. Everything in her life seemed to depend on whether she'd see a slight, youthful figure in a rumpled white jacket at a scarred wooden table just where the corridor made a right-angle bend.

"The room boy's there," she said breathlessly.

"So?"

"So we're saying good night at my door." Her voice was firm. She would not openly flout her host country's standards.

"With what—a handshake? I think you're being silly, Gillian."

"Silly or not, it's better than taking a chance."

So after a smile and good night to the room boy and the long walk down the hall, they exchanged one quick kiss at her door and he left her. Alone once more, she leaned her head against the closed door. She would see him again tomorrow. A warm, happy feeling spread through her. What a bright flame love made!

chapter 9

THE SCENE BEING shot the next day was of the makeshift hospital in the British Legation, a room with sandbagged windows and clouds of mosquito netting, where the wounded of all nationalities lay on straw-filled mattresses on the floor. The characters played by Andrea and Robyn were serving as nurses, along with a number of women missionaries. Robyn, the girl the lieutenant eventually marries, was to become hysterical under the onslaught of the wounded crying out in different languages for water, the overpowering heat of the room, and the hopelessness of being rescued. Andrea was to slap Robyn to bring her back to her senses. Robyn would then stand off and accuse Andrea of jealousy because Andrea's lover, the lieutenant, had paid some attention to Robyn.

Gillian watched while the extras donned hospital gowns made of silk drapes, damask tablecloths, and bright Chinese cottons, which the legation ladies, who had had no other materials, had improvised.

Then Dan was yelling, "Silence!" A Chinese interpreter barked *"An Jing!"* through a bullhorn.

Next, it was "Prepare!" and *"Yu Bei!"*

When the "Action!" call came, the cameras started to roll on the wounded in their strange garb, with bandages made of bags of sawdust. The only lights in the night scene were small lanterns covered with dark cloth that the nurses carried and then placed on the floor with the light to the wall, because occasionally a bullet came whistling through.

The script called for a sweating, overworked Robyn to be walking down the narrow aisle between the straw pallets, when a Sikh soldier, an Indian in a bloodstained turban, unable to make himself understood, would pull at her skirt and gesture for water. Her nerves on edge, she would scream.

But time after time, an exasperated Burke yelled "Cut!" He walked over to the blonde actress and said, "Robyn, sweetheart, that scream's gotta do more. It's still too tame. You're at the end of your rope, ready to go over the brink. You've had it. Have you ever felt like that in real life?"

"That's the way I feel now," Robyn said flatly.

Burke stared at her a moment, obviously not sure how to take this. "Okay, so give me a primal scream right from your gut."

Robyn screamed till Burke was satisfied. He yelled "Take five!" and the cameras rolled again. Robyn entered the ward, the Sikh clutched at her skirt, she screamed, Andrea slapped her, the two women argued, a bullet whistled overhead, and Andrea protected Robyn with her body. The danger over, they fell sobbing in each other's arms.

It wasn't till Burke yelled gleefully, "It's a wrap!" that Gillian realized what had been nagging her throughout the just-completed filming. She debated with herself whether she should tell Burke, now that the scene had been shot. Then she decided she had to. It was too important to ignore.

"The scene's got a problem, Burke," she said hesitantly.

"Oh, yeah? What?"

"The Sikh never got his drink of water, did he?"

"That's the script girl's responsibility. Holy damn! Is everybody asleep on the set or is she off somewhere with Dan? Why didn't you tell me that before? We must have rehearsed the thing three times, not counting Robyn's scream."

"I'm sorry. I really am. My mind was on something else, I'm afraid."

"Your mind should be on your work all the time, not just when you feel like it. That's what separates the men from the boys, or maybe women from men."

"That's unfair, and you know it. You're just taking your frustrations with the scene out on me."

Burke laughed. "That's a wife's line. We're not married, Gillian."

His laugh infuriated her. "That's fine with me, because it just so happens I don't feel like speaking a wife's lines—to put it in Hollywoodese. Not now or ever!"

"Very dramatic. Maybe we'll use *you* in that scene instead of Robyn. You can also give the Sikh a drink of water. And if you think of anything else, please tell me *before* we start shooting next time."

"I'll try to remember," she said sarcastically.

"Thanks. I'll send you an invitation to the Academy Awards dinner."

"What for? To see you get the empty envelope for Best Director of the Year?"

"There's no award for Best Historical Consultant."

"How would Hollywood *know?*" Gillian asked contemptuously.

"Let's cut it out, Gillian. We've got an audience."

Gillian looked around and saw the grinning cast and

crew. She also had a glimpse of Andrea's face before the regal mask slipped back into place. The beautiful features had been distorted with jealousy as she stared at Gillian.

For a moment she wondered if Andrea's interest in Burke was solely romantic. Then Gillian glanced toward Robyn. She was only a few years younger than the star. They must have known each other before Andrea dropped out of films. Robyn's drunken comment when they first met, about Andrea's being able to wrap Burke around her little finger, came back to her. What had Robyn said afterward? Something about Andrea's always coming out on top, no matter what it took. *Why* could Andrea wrap Burke around her little finger? Did Robyn know?

At the moment Robyn was having problems of her own. Even now, when she had stopped drinking and her acting had improved, Burke never seemed satisfied with her performance. And, although Gillian liked Robyn and considered her a friend, she had to admit Burke was right. Robyn was no actress. How she had lasted in Hollywood as long as she had, even in secondary roles, was something Gillian didn't want to think about.

The two women—Robyn and Andrea—were now really arguing. Robyn accused Andrea of actually slapping her instead of just fanning her cheek so the motion would look like a slap. Andrea retorted with insults about Robyn's acting ability. With a disgusted look, Burke sent Dan over to mediate, and it occurred to Gillian that all their nerves were getting a little ragged. It was no secret that Robyn and Andrea didn't get along, but this was the first time their animosity had broken out into open warfare. And Burke was definitely on edge.

She watched him as he came striding across the set to her again. Burke never just walked, Gillian mused. He strode or bounded or stalked. And as always when he was working, his face wore an expression of total absorption. But now, after the frustrations of the last scene, the angular lines of his face were more pronounced, and his forehead was furrowed with worry.

"We're going to the Ming Tombs." He put his hand out and took her by the arm. "C'mon."

"It's lunchtime," Gillian wailed, "and I'm hungry."

"I'll have Dan order us box lunches at the Tombs."

"How about this afternoon's scenes?"

"One of my assistant directors will take over."

He dropped her arm and was already crossing the set to one of the company's cars. As Gillian hurried to catch up with him, a faint smile on her face, she caught another glimpse of Andrea. Robyn was talking earnestly with Dan—at least *that* old feud had ended—and Andrea was standing apart from them, staring at Gillian with a bitter look again.

"Why the Ming Tombs?" Gillian asked as they seated themselves in the back of Keng's Shanghai.

"Remember you told me the ladies and gentlemen of the legations used to go out there and have picnics on moonlit nights?"

Gillian smiled and nodded. Burke might snap at her now and then, as he did at everybody when the tension was too great, but at least he now respected her professional knowledge.

"I've decided to include a scene like that. It'll happen early in the story, before the siege, of course. It'll mark the beginning of the affair between the lieutenant and the woman. We're going to shoot it tonight."

"Why at night instead of in the daytime? Why aren't you using day-for-night?" Gillian was showing off a little, proud of her newly acquired knowledge of film vocabulary and techniques.

"Because night-for-night is more convincing. I want this scene to convey an impression of innocence. It's before the siege. The Westerners know the Boxer movement is growing, but not for a minute do they think they could actually be in danger from these fanatics, so they go out to the Ming Tombs for a moonlight picnic as usual, and flirt and gossip and joke about the Boxers. We're using pale blue gels to give the light a slightly bluish cast," he added, further initiating Gillian in the mysteries of the trade. "Then, at the end, there's a dramatic bit where the wind blows open the shirt of one of their trusted servants, and the insignia of the Boxer, a red sash, is revealed."

"It sounds wonderful," Gillian said. "I can just see them in their lovely white clothes, with their Chinese servants and huge picnic hampers."

"I think it'll work," Burke agreed.

"But why are we going out there now?"

"I want to look around before Grossman and the rest of the crew get out here. I also want any input you'd care to give me. You can start by filling me in a little on the background."

Sitting well away from Burke, Gillian started her recital in a dry, matter-of-fact voice. "The Valley of the Thirteen Ming Tombs is the burial place of all but three of the Ming emperors, along with their wives and favorite concubines. The site was chosen because it's backed by foothills and mountains, which would protect the corpse of the emperor from evil spirits carried by the northern wind."

"There's a lot of north wind right here in the back seat," Burke said with a grin. "I'm not saying anything about evil spirits, just that it's definitely chilly."

"You're a little hard on Robyn, aren't you, Burke? She's stopped drinking since she got together with Phil, and I guess her work's improved, at least it looks that way to me, so why are you still so impatient with her?" And why so everlastingly patient with Andrea? Gillian added to herself.

Burke was silent awhile. Looking at the new lines of fatigue in his face, the clenched jaw, and downward-drooping lines of his mouth, Gillian was sorry she had spoken. But only for a moment. What she had said was true. Burke wasn't fair to Robyn. What was more, Gillian half-hoped that out of this discussion some explanation of his overly protective attitude toward Andrea would emerge.

He turned to her, and his blue eyes had that honest, clear look she liked so well. "You're right, I don't have the patience with Robyn I should have, but maybe it's myself I'm angry at for having cast Robyn in that part in the first place. Frankly, she's not much of an actress. It was Andrea who wanted her, and I gave in to Andrea."

There it was—Andrea again. And why would Andrea have wanted Robyn in the cast when neither woman could stand the sight of the other?

"Then your dissatisfaction with Robyn isn't because she's too old to play the young girl," Gillian said slowly. "I thought that might be it—partly, at least."

Burke looked surprised. "No, Robyn's not much more than thirty. With makeup and lighting, she looks the part all right."

But because she didn't have the advantage of real youth and because she wasn't a talented actress, Robyn couldn't be a threat to Andrea. And that was why the star had wanted her. Surely Burke, so astute about everything else, saw that.

To test his reaction, Gillian said, "I suppose Andrea thought Robyn wouldn't be competition for her."

All expression disappeared from Burke's face, as if it were a child's magic slate rubbed clean.

"Tell me more about the Ming Tombs, Gillian." His tone was lightly ironic; his eyes, bright with amusement.

Obviously he had caught on to the fact that she was fishing, and just as obviously he wasn't going to say anything about Andrea. So Gillian continued to dispense information about the tombs while she wondered why questions about his ex-wife were taboo.

"We're coming to the Sacred Way now, the approach to the Valley of the Tombs. This is the famous Avenue of Animals."

The massive stone statues of animals, arranged as

equidistant pairs on both sides of the road, were awe-
inspiring. Six animals were represented—two different
mythical beasts, a camel, an elephant, a lion, and a
horse—and each was shown in both a standing and
kneeling position. There were twelve statues on each side
of the road, twenty-four in all.

"Wow!" Burke exclaimed. "What a sight! I want to
include *this* in the picnic scene. Just think what those
statues will look like in the moonlight."

"Wait." Gillian smiled at his enthusiasm. "There's
more to come."

A little farther along, the Sacred Way turned to the
right and revealed a row of sculptures of humans. Again
they were in pairs, one on each side of the road—two
military mandarins with swords, two civilian mandarins
holding tablets, and two retired mandarins.

"What are these stone figures for?" Burke asked.

"No one's quite sure, but it is believed the animals
were put there to guard the dead emperor and his wives
in the next world, and the human figures to serve them."

"That could be. All of them seem benevolent."

Trust Burke to observe that, Gillian thought, and to
stop a moment when they got out of the car to look
around him at the beauty of the site. The plum trees were
in flower, the delicacy of their pink-and-white blossoms
set off by the bluish pine trees around them. The dull
color of the trees formed a perfect backdrop as well for
the ochre-red pavilions, with their upturned yellow roofs.

A professional photographer had set up shop outside
one of the tombs. He had the customary paraphernalia:
a large blue umbrella, a card table bearing a glass vase
of artificial red roses, and an old-fashioned camera. He
sat apathetically on a folding chair behind the table, waiting for business.

"Do you want to go into the tomb?" Gillian asked.
"There's not much left to see, but it's worth a visit."

"If we can do it fast. I want to walk around the grounds
awhile before Phil and the others come."

They descended the three flights of stairs leading into the tomb and looked at the two six-inch-thick marble doors that had once separated the two chambers of the tomb. The doors were on display along the wall together with a "locking stone," which fit into a slot in the floor and would slide down to lock the door from the inside. They looked briefly at the altars of the emperor and empress and the throne with the carved dragon.

Then Burke said, "Let's go. We'll take a quick tour of the place, then have lunch."

Gillian was silent as Burke walked about, examining pavilions and lawns and pine groves for possible settings. She knew it was the way he worked. He had to absorb himself totally in a scene before he could even begin to discuss it.

That abstracted, faraway look was still in his eyes when he grabbed her hand and said, "C'mon. Let's pick up those box lunches and eat. I'm starved, and you must be too. Where do we go?"

They walked past the pavilions to a utilitarian building with picnic tables and benches. This was where tour groups visiting the Ming Tombs were brought for their lunch. Stacks of plain white cardboard boxes were waiting on a counter. Gillian identified herself to the woman in charge and was given two boxes, which they took outside.

They sat in the sunshine on a low concrete wall surrounding a flower bed. Gingerly Gillian started to open her box, while Burke watched.

"I'm afraid to look," he said glumly.

Gillian laughed. "This isn't a box lunch. It's a smorgasbord. Look!"

The box contained chicken wings, the usual doughy spring rolls, which had about as much spring as feather pillows, roast pork buns, a small cake, an apple, a pint bottle of Lao Shan, the Chinese mineral water, and a tissue-thin paper napkin.

"It's just like a church social," Burke commented.

"Chicken and biscuits and soda pop."

"If it were a church social, would you bid for my box?"

"Not if I knew you cooked like this," he grumbled.

When they finished eating, they sat awhile in the mild sunshine. Burke put his hand over Gillian's as it rested on the sun-warmed stone. Even so slight a touch electrified her. She could feel the strength and energy in his fingers as they curled around hers. He separated her fingers and ran his index finger lightly along the inside of them, barely grazing the skin, titillating her nerves into a heightened receptivity that magnified her pleasure. She wanted to purr and rub herself against him like a cat in the warm sun.

A cloud of dust swirled over a nearby field. Gillian blinked. For a second she had thought it was the dust-making machine they used on the set. She grimaced wryly. After only a short while with the film company, she couldn't distinguish the real from the artificial.

"Tinseltown." That's what Hollywood was called. Was it love, or sexual passion, Burke felt for her? He had never said he loved her. But she knew she loved him. She also knew they were bonded together, that, loving or fighting, they alone were a match for each other. And she knew that she wanted him to do things to her she never thought of with other men.

She glanced at him. His mind wasn't on her, she knew. It was on *Siege*. He looked at his watch.

"We'd better go," he said. "I'm supposed to meet them at the entrance. You can go back to Peking in the car. All we'll be doing is technical stuff, anyway. You'll return for the night shooting, okay?"

Two buses were parked on the road. People Gillian recognized were still stepping down out of one of them, while the grips were unloading equipment from the other.

On her way to Keng's car, she waved at Phil Grossman and some of the others. To her surprise, Phil's wave was perfunctory, and his smile looked as though it required a painful effort.

Gillian had a feeling of foreboding. The accumulated tension of weeks of hard, unrelenting work was beginning to show. They all relied on one another so much, if one of them gave way, it would be bad for the entire company.

As for herself, she wanted nothing more than the free afternoon that lay ahead—time she could spend writing letters, doing her nails, fixing a hem. Time in which she'd try very hard not to think of Burke Ferrara, of the one thrilling night they had had together, and the very real possibility that there would never be another.

Late in the afternoon, Gillian grew tired of her own company and decided to pay Robyn a visit. But her knock at Robyn's door brought a slurred, mumbled response that sent fear to Gillian's heart.

"It's Gillian," she said softly.

"Go 'way, Gillie. I don't wan'a visit."

Gillian swallowed hard. There was no doubt that Robyn had been drinking and with only a short time left before the company had to board the bus for the trip out to the Ming Tombs, the situation was very bad indeed.

"I'm coming in," she called out, and pushed open the door.

Robyn was curled up on her bed, fully clothed. Her eyes were red and swollen, her face tear-streaked. Her wavy blond hair was tangled and messy. A bottle of Scotch and a teacup crowded out a box of Kleenex on the bedside table.

"I told you not to come in, Gillie," she said reproachfully.

"I had to see if you were all right."

"Well, now that you've seen, you can leave. Okay?"

There was more bravado in Robyn's voice than real anger. Gillian also noted with relief that Robyn was less drunk than she had at first thought.

Suddenly an image of Phil's grim expression and curt wave flashed before her. She sat down on the edge of the bed and took Robyn's hand.

"Is it Phil?" Gillian said softly.

The actress nodded. Her pretty face was contorted with unhappiness.

"He saw me and Dan kidding around together and got mad."

Gillian smiled. "Jealousy just means he cares."

At this Robyn shook her head violently, and tears welled up in her baby-blue eyes.

"He called me a name. I yelled back at him, and we had a terrible fight."

She was crying in earnest now, and Gillian reached automatically for the box of tissues and put it in front of her friend.

Gillian could well imagine the name Phil had used and how that would have hurt Robyn, considering her newfound joy in Phil's love. She stroked Robyn's hand, knowing that the best thing for the actress now was to cry out her hurt. At the same time she wondered if Robyn would be able to play her scene that night. Even if the makeup artists could repair the ravages to her face, would she be sober and calm enough to concentrate on her lines?

Finally her sobbing slowed, then stopped. Robyn blew her nose vigorously and stared seriously at Gillian through reddened eyes.

"I love him so much, Gillie. I couldn't bear to lose him. He's the only decent guy I've ever known who liked me too." She hiccuped on another sob, then went on. "I was going to quit acting. I know I'm no actress, for God's sake. We were going to have a baby . . . to replace the children he . . ."

"Lost," Gillian finished for her as Robyn broke out in fresh sobs. "I know, and I think that may explain Phil's reaction to you and Dan."

That stopped Robyn. She blew her nose again and looked up at Gillian with intense interest.

"What do you mean?"

"I think that terrible loss Phil suffered made him afraid of losing a loved one again. Phil's a sophisticated man. Ordinarily he wouldn't even react to a Don Juan like Dan paying a little attention to the woman he loves. But he's been sensitized, so to speak. He overreacts to the threat of loss. And that's why he blew up. And you know, Robyn, people say a lot of things when they're mad that they don't mean."

A smile spread over Robyn's face. "Do you really think that was it, Gillie?"

"I don't know for sure. Nothing's sure in life. But yes, I think that's why Phil reacted as he did. Maybe you'll find out on the set tonight."

"The set! My God, Gillie, I can't show up tonight looking like this." Forcing the words out, she added, "I've been drinking, too."

"You don't say!"

"Just two," Robyn said defensively.

"To be on the safe side, let's get some hot coffee into you. Then bathe your face in cold water and take a shower. With a lot of makeup, you should be all right."

"You think so, Gillie?" The actress looked anxiously at Gillian. "I'm afraid of Burke," she confessed in a little girl's voice. "He'll skin me alive if I show up under the influence."

"He'll skin you alive if you don't show up, period. Why don't you splash cold water on your face while I make some instant coffee? Then take a shower."

"All right, Gillie," the actress said obediently.

Gillian took a cup and spooned out two heaping teaspoons of powdered coffee from an almost empty jar. Then she poured hot boiled water from the thermos over it and stirred the dark mixture.

She moved slowly, with a feeling of dread. Her worry about Robyn had expanded to include the whole company. She had heard that nighttime shooting was always difficult. She wondered if they were up to it, after so many weeks of hard work. She wished Burke had thought of the scene earlier in the shooting schedule when the actors were newly arrived on location and more refreshed.

When Robyn emerged from the bathroom, her face shiny and red from the cold water, Gillian handed her the cup of hot coffee, and Robyn sat down to drink it.

It wasn't just the overwork that was making members of the company edgy with one another, Gillian mused. There were emotional problems—Burke's displeasure with Robyn, Phil and Robyn's quarrel, Andrea's newly surfacing hostility toward her, Gillian. She could go on with the list, Gillian thought wearily, but there was no point. Her immediate job was to help Robyn get herself in shape so she could work that night.

The blond actress had taken several slurps of the coffee and was watching Gillian over the rim of the cup. "You're a real friend, you know that, Gillie?"

Gillian smiled and shrugged it off. "You'd do the same for me, wouldn't you?"

"Yeah, 'cept you'd never get yourself in the kind of fixes I do. You're always so cool and controlled."

Cool and controlled. That was a laugh! Had there been a single day since she met Burke Ferrara when her emotions hadn't been churned up?

"Except where Burke's concerned," Robyn continued, a sly look on her face and an amused glint in her eyes.

Protocol called for an exchange of confidences, but Gillian didn't want to talk about Burke. Coupled with her own rather acute sense of privacy was the feeling that she could never convey the complexity of her emotions or of the situation that existed between her and Burke Ferrara.

So she remained silent, aware that a faint expression of pain had crossed her face. Robyn must have noticed it too. She reached forward and put her hand on Gillian's.

"Maybe someday I can repay you, Gillie...with a little information." She stopped talking then and, giving Gillian's hand a final pat, stood up. "I've got to get going. You do too. You're going to change, aren't you?"

Gillian glanced down abstractedly at the green velour lounge suit she had put on. What "information" did Robyn have for her? If she hadn't found Robyn in such a bad way, she would probably have pumped her about Andrea and Burke. Was that the information Robyn meant? Whatever it was, the time to hear it had passed. Robyn was on her determined way to the bathroom, and Gillian had to leave to get ready.

Gillian dressed for the night's work in white pedal pushers, a yellow-and-white-striped jersey, and loafers. She knotted a bright yellow Shetland wool cardigan around her throat for warmth later on in the night and let her hair fall free over her shoulders.

A knock on her door announced a completely transformed Robyn. Whatever she had done in the way of makeup and other techniques had worked wonders. Not only were there no signs of her recent tears, but her face even had a fresh, dewy look.

At Gillian's look of pleased surprise, Robyn said with wide-eyed honesty, "I'm going to try to make up with Phil." For a second her face darkened with anger. "Damn that beach bum, Ross, anyway. I almost think he got me in trouble with Phil on purpose, out of meanness or boredom or something. I knew he was no good in the first place."

The cast and crew had been provided with the usual Ming Tomb box lunch for supper. Gillian made a face as she opened the box and looked at the same fare she had had just a few hours ago. But she ate it, because it looked like it would be a long night.

She was glad when one of the assistant directors asked her to do the interpreting for some Chinese technicians who hadn't worked with the company before. It gave her something active to do rather than just passively watching the preparations for the night's filming.

Also it got her away from the overly tense principals on the set. Burke had been so absorbed in what he was doing, he hadn't even noticed she was there. His eyes were darkly serious as he rehearsed the actors. Every bone in his face stood out under the harsh bright lights. Andrea looked lovely as ever, in a white cotton batiste shirtwaist with small covered buttons and a long white skirt, flounced at the hem. And Robyn, Gillian was glad to see, was her usual fluffily blond self, in a similar costume. But whereas Andrea fiddled incessantly with her mesh gloves, pulling them off and putting them on again, Robyn showed her nervousness by continually patting her hair. She also, Gillian noticed, kept glancing toward Phil. But what his response was, Gillian couldn't see.

When she had finished helping the technicians, Gillian returned to the glaringly bright set and stood in the shadows to watch the rehearsal. The scene was a charming one—the elegant ladies and distinguished-looking men of the legations talking and laughing in the moonlight while their white-garbed Chinese servants discreetly passed among them, serving the sumptuous picnic supper. Later, Gillian knew, the lieutenant would draw the heroine, played by Andrea, away from the crowd and into the red and gold pavilion so they could be alone.

She noticed suddenly that on the fringes of the group, two Sikhs stood, turbaned, bearded, and in uniform, as if guarding the picnickers. She felt a twinge of dismay. This hadn't been in the script and wasn't right. But before she could do anything about it, Burke's voice roared out over the set.

"What the hell are those two Sikhs doing there?" Burke bellowed.

Everyone turned to look. There were some muttered "I don't knows" and "don't ask mes." Then Andrea's cool, fluty tones rang out. "I believe Gillian decided it would look more realistic if we had guards. You know, in case the Boxers attacked."

Gillian stood transfixed, hardly believing what she had just heard. Her suspension of belief continued through Burke's outraged yell, "Gillian! Where the hell are you? What was the big idea...?"

She snapped out of it then and stepped into the lighted area. She blinked in the intense light, feeling like the object of a third-degree police interrogation.

Gillian had just started an indignant "But I didn't—" when Andrea smoothly interrupted with, "At least I think that was Gillian's intention. You were there, Dan. Was that the impression you had too?"

She could almost see the wheels turn in Dan's head. If he backed up the star, it could mean a world of career opportunities for him. And what real harm would it do Gillian? he would rationalize.

Gillian felt sick with disgust. It was beneath her dignity even to defend herself against such a blatant lie. Moreover Burke had believed Andrea. He hadn't even waited for Dan to support her accusation. He had lit into Gillian on the strength of Andrea's word alone.

Not deigning to look at him, she stood and let his waves of abuse crash around her head. From time to time she absorbed his words—"unwarranted interference," "meddling," "stupid idea"—but most of the time she closed her ears to the harsh, berating voice—the voice of the man she had once loved.

He finally came to the end of his tirade. Wearily he said, "Get those Sikhs out of here. And let me repeat, for anyone who still doesn't understand, that the whole purpose of this scene is to show that the Westerners feel secure in their little world, that they don't *expect* to be attacked. Then the camera cuts to the man in the red sash—the secret Boxer, the trusted servant, the enemy right in their midst. The scene is ironic. The whole purpose is destroyed by having the picnic party post guards."

And with a final fling of sarcasm: "I don't see how *anybody* could miss that point."

When the business of shooting the scene recommenced, Gillian melted into the shadows and walked quickly through the grounds to the entrance of the Ming Tombs site. Keng was there, and she asked him to take her to the White Cloud Hotel.

She sat forward on the comfortable gray upholstery, her hands balled up into fists, her nails digging into her palms. Her whole being was shaken with a sense of outrage and betrayal. Keng looked at her solicitously, then quietly closed the glass divider. She was free now to cry in privacy.

But she didn't. She was too stunned and too angry to cry. Image after image of the faces that had surrounded her flashed through her mind. Andrea's triumphant smile, Dan's uneasy expression as he lied, Burke's storm-furrowed brow, Robyn's open amazement.

Then slowly the anger flowed out of her. Left behind was an emptiness that felt like freedom. Nobody could blame her if she left Peking now. Nobody would even expect her to stay after a public humiliation like the one to which Burke had submitted her. Most important of all, she wouldn't blame herself. Persisting in her hopeless love for Burke now would be masochistic, not the free choice of an independent, autonomous woman.

She'd pack her bags tonight and see about travel arrangements tomorrow. The film was almost done anyway. A prewrap party had even been planned for tomorrow night. Even if they hadn't been close to the end, she would have had to leave. She couldn't possibly work with Andrea or Dan or Burke again. With a short, harsh laugh, she reflected on the irony of her situation. Only a few hours after she had assured Robyn of Phil's love, her own love affair had been torched in a matter of minutes.

chapter 10

SOMETIME THAT NIGHT she woke up to the sound of her door being opened and softly closed.

"I'm all right, Robyn," she murmured, her tone muffled and nasal from the wild bouts of crying that had followed her return to her room. "I just want to sleep."

She felt her bed sag under a weight. Annoyed, yet touched by her friend's solicitude, Gillian put out her hand and said, "I'm leaving Peking. I'm all packed. But I'll say goodbye tomorrow."

When a hand—too large for Robyn's—closed around hers, she opened her mouth to scream, but the hand moved to her mouth, covering it, and a familiar voice said, "Don't, Gillian. It's me, Burke." He took his hand away then and laid it gently on her arm.

"Get out!" she whispered violently. "This minute! Or I *will* scream, and believe me, you and your star and your whole stinking company will be thrown out of China."

"Don't!" he pleaded. "I know how you feel, but—"

"Oh, no, you don't. You couldn't. When have *you* ever been shocked by dishonesty or lies or betrayal?"

"I'm terribly sorry to have said those things to you in public, Gillian. But we're all pretty much at the end of our rope, myself included. And when I saw those Sikhs on the set, I just blew up. I couldn't understand why you had brought them in. *You* of all people! You knew the significance of the scene, the ironic point I was trying to make. Why *did* you insist on having the Sikhs there?"

Gillian stiffened under the bedclothes. She had already packed her pajamas and had gone to bed in her teddy. As a result of her vigorous movement, she could feel the champagne-colored satin rippling across her breasts.

She could tell Burke his misconception involved a lie, that she had been framed by Andrea and Dan Ross. But she didn't care what he thought of her any longer. It wouldn't make any difference anyway. Andrea could tear up all the scripts, smash the cameras, burn the dressing trailers, and he wouldn't say "boo." Why? Because she was Andrea. There was no sense of logic or truth or justice to the man.

When she remained silent, he said, "Well, you don't have to tell me if you don't want to. I'll give the studio a good report on you anyway."

She exploded then. That condescending tone of his goaded her into fury, as it always did—as, indeed, he had to have known it would. She wanted to hurt him in every way she could, physically and in his arrogant ego and his deceiving heart.

Violently she shot her legs forward in a kick and had the satisfaction of hearing him grunt with pain. She sat up and threw herself on him, aiming punches at his face and chest. He grabbed her hands, but she broke free. This time she clawed at him like a cat, and knew she had hurt him when he winced again.

"Why, you little hellcat," he said, dropping her hands and putting his own to his cheek. "You've drawn blood!"

This was her chance to escape. She started to swing herself out of bed, but he was too fast for her. He seized her ankles, so that she couldn't move.

She could still fight, though. Her punches might be weak, but she could scratch and hurt and draw blood.

"Let me go!" she hissed, and reached for his face again.

"Oh no, not again. Once is enough." Releasing her ankles, he grabbed her wrists and pinioned her hands above her head.

The same moon that had lit the Ming Tombs let her see his face as he bent over her, and the sight of the face that had become so dear to her forced her to turn away to hide her anguish.

But she would not be spiritless. The only way out of a bad situation was to go straight through it. She turned back to him. Eyes flashing, breasts heaving under the champagne satin with the force of her fury, she said, "Let me go, Burke. My bags are packed, and I'm leaving tomorrow. It's finished. So all this is silly."

"I told you the first time we went out that I wouldn't let you screw up my film *and* keep me out of your bed. For some unknown reason, you seem intent on doing both. I'm staying till you tell me why."

Holding her small wrists with one hand, he slowly passed the other across her bare shoulders, over her satin-soft breast, and down the full length of her, cupping her rounded hip and trailing one finger along the inside of her thigh.

She tried to hold herself rigid and unyielding so he wouldn't know what effect he was having on her. But as he stroked and touched her, she quivered with mounting excitement.

"Will you tell me, Gillian," he said, "or will I have to kiss you to force it out of you?"

"You! You!" She couldn't think of an epithet low enough for him. Gillian tried to twist her long, slender legs free, but he had adroitly pinned them down with his weight so she couldn't kick him. Now he took advantage of her movement to cover more of her body with his.

"And please note, I didn't say *where* I'd have to kiss you."

He pulled one slim shoulder strap down, then touched the soft swell of her breast with his mouth.

"All right, I'll tell you. She was lying," Gillian said with fury. "Your Andrea set me up. I didn't order those Sikhs on the set. She did. Then she blamed me and got Dan to support her."

He sat up and looked down into her face but without freeing her.

"That's a pretty serious accusation."

"Obviously it's my word against hers, or to be more exact, hers and Dan's. But do you really think I'd be so stupid as to destroy the whole meaning of your scene?"

He dropped her wrists then and shifted his weight off her feet. "No. That's why I couldn't understand why you would have brought the Sikhs in. I thought you did it on purpose, but why, I didn't know."

"On purpose!"

"I told you directors—or at least this director—have a tendency toward paranoia by the end of a film. I'm doubly sorry, Gillian. What I said to you was bad enough, but to say it unjustly, when it wasn't true!" He put his head in his hands. "God, what a chump I've been!"

She longed to run her hands through his dark hair and pull his head onto her breast, to feel his weight on her and his smooth back under the palms of her hands. But she didn't move.

In a quiet, still voice, she said, "What's Andrea to you, Burke?"

His answer came quick and sure. "Nothing. My ex-wife, that's all."

He reached for her then, murmuring, "Gillian, you're the one I . . ."

But she pushed him away and swung her legs down,

then stood in a shaft of moonlight, straight as a silver arrow.

"I wish you'd go now, Burke. Really. The whole thing's been too much. I don't want any more of it."

It was true. She never had headaches, but a throbbing like a jackhammer breaking up the sidewalk had started, and she felt she literally would not be able to withstand another onslaught on her emotions.

"Will you stay, though, Gillian?" he asked.

"I don't know," she answered dully. She wasn't playing hard to get or waiting for him to coax her into staying. She had already mentally prepared herself to leave. With a tremendous effort of will she had wrenched her mind away from thoughts of Burke and focused them on the classes she'd be teaching next semester at Haywood and the research project she was eager to start.

The only thing she didn't think about was her apartment just off campus. It had seemed like heaven after she divorced Elliot—her own place, which she had furnished in a comfortable, welcoming style. Now when she pictured it, briefly, room by attractive room, it looked lonely as hell.

"I need you," he said humbly.

It shocked Gillian to hear Burke plead like that. She wanted the old caustic, cocksure, crazy Burke Ferrara back. But Gillian would not be swayed.

"You'd better keep Andrea and Dan out of my way. I'm afraid I'll vomit if I have to look at them."

"Aren't you getting a little carried away? Andrea's used to the no-holds-barred ethics of Hollywood, and Dan's type is everywhere—the weak, ambitious young man who'll do anything to get ahead. I don't condone what they did, but it's not the first time vengeful or insecure people have resorted to dirty tricks."

Gillian stared at him in amazement. Were there no lengths to which he would not go to protect Andrea?

"If that's the way you play ball, I'm on the wrong

team. I'm leaving tomorrow. Good night, Burke."

He stood up then and took her by the shoulders. His fingers bit into her flesh. He gave her a little shake, and her shoulder strap fell again. She reached to pull it up, but he said curtly, "Leave it!"

She looked up into his face. His eyes were like blue flames; his lean jaw was tight with anger.

"*I* don't play ball like that. I was only trying to explain to you that other people do. I'm sorry Andrea did that to you. I think it was reprehensible of her, and I may tell her so tomorrow. Or I may not. And don't forget, what she did was an offense against me, her director, as well as against you. But the show must go on. We've got to finish the film. And if you're any kind of a professional, you'll stay to the bitter end, Gillian," he finished tauntingly.

"Bitter" was correct, she thought. She'd bet all the tea in China that Burke wouldn't reprimand Andrea. But his appeal to her professionalism was an effective one. She prided herself on being a pro in every way.

"I'll stay," she said stiffly. "And I'll work with Andrea and Dan if I have to. But I want you to go now, Burke. As I said before, I've pretty much had it for one night."

As she turned toward the window, she heard the door close quietly behind her. Her glance fell on her bags. Strapped and zipped shut, they looked as they had the day she arrived, when Gillian wondered whether she should unpack them and stay or go back to Boston. With a wry smile she told herself, "'Tis better to have loved and lost, than never to have loved at all," and went to bed.

When Gillian walked onto the set the next day, she sensed an unspoken support from members of the film company. People went out of their way to smile or talk to her. Phil Grossman gave her a big bear hug. One of the grips shyly brought her a cup of coffee during the mid-morning break. Even Trent Baylor, the Cold Fish, gave her a giant wink and a thumb's up signal.

Robyn provided the explanation. Without saying a word she handed Gillian a mimeographed sheet. It was a memo from Burke to all members of the company, advising them that he had apologized to Gillian West for mistakenly accusing her of an improper action in connection with the filming of *Siege*.

"Thanks, Robyn," Gillian said.

"Maybe you should thank Burke. He didn't go to bed last night, getting that thing out. Neither did Dan. I understand Burke got him up and made him run the mimeograph machine. But Dan had it coming to him. Too bad we couldn't do something to Andrea for starting the big lie."

Robyn's eyes were so serious, her whole demeanor so grave, that unconsciously Gillian glanced toward Phil.

At that, Robyn broke into a smile. "We made up. Everything's all right with us again."

Gillian put her hand over her friend's. "I'm so glad, Robyn."

Robyn nodded happily. "Are you going to thank him now?"

Gillian didn't answer. She had been avoiding Burke all morning. Avoidance, however, was not her tactic when it came to Andrea and Dan. She had marched right past them, her eyes flashing with scorn, her lips curled in contempt.

Dan had shrunk back from her, shamefaced. Andrea had looked through her regally, as though Gillian weren't there.

Thanking a person for something done on your behalf was a civilized act, and Gillian believed in such basic courtesies. So, nervously pulling down her red-and-white-striped knit top and tugging at the waistband of her poppy-red culottes, she started across the set to Burke. He was standing apart from the other coffee drinkers, stroking a cup nervously with his long fingers and gazing thoughtfully into the distance.

That's my Burke, Gillian told herself. My clever, determined-to-have-his-own-way, slightly unscrupulous Burke. He's put Robyn up to showing me the memo, and now he's waiting for me to come to him.

Then he started toward her, his faded plaid flannel shirt open at his tanned throat, the swing of his walk easy and free, his blue eyes sapphire-clear. Gillian's heart started pounding again, her mouth went dry, and every feeling in her rose to the surface, eager to be touched in some way by this man.

"I thought you'd never come," he said lightly, mockingly.

"Simple courtesy requires that I thank you for the memo," she answered with a shrug.

"Ah, Simple Courtesy, I know her well. She's a cold, pale thing. Nothing at all like Heartfelt Warmth or Heady Passion, my favorite Hungarian actress." His smile broadened into a grin. "May I take you to the prewrap party tonight? I understand there's going to be dancing to disco records no more than five years old, and egg rolls, and whatever the cast and crew can scrape up in the way of booze, which should be considerable."

"Won't having the boss there put a crimp in their style?"

"Not this boss. You've got to come, Gillian. If you don't, they'll think you're mad at me, and that'll be bad for company morale," Burke cajoled.

"And I suppose you'll send a bad report about me to the studio," she said sarcastically.

Burke flippantly responded, "Absolutely. And you'll never get another job as a film consultant in China."

"Gee! That would be devastating."

Suddenly the joking stopped, and Burke's intensely blue eyes held hers in a challenge—a challenge she couldn't refuse. "Will you come?"

"Of course. I adore egg rolls."

* * *

Dress for the party would be casual, Gillian knew. Fortunately she had brought with her a boat-neck T-shirt dress in a salmon-pink knit. It was slit up the side and had roll-up sleeves, with gold-tone grommets laced with satin cord at the shoulders.

To make the dress look less sporty, she wore sheer hose and high-heeled pumps. And because it was a party, she applied evening makeup and *Magie Noire*, her "signature" perfume. Then she brushed her hair into soft waves that fell to her shoulders. Finally, she considered earrings, then decided against them, and simply wore her heavy gold bracelets.

The look in Burke's eyes when she opened her door to his knock was worth all her efforts. He even sniffed at her appreciatively and would have bent forward for a kiss, but she put her hand out and stopped him.

On the way down to the tea lounge, on the main floor of the hotel, Gillian said, "Why a prewrap party? I've only heard of wrap parties, to celebrate the end of a film."

"Right. But everyone's getting restless now that we're so close to the finish line. They've done everything there is to do in Peking—they've gone to the Peking Opera, the circus, the ballet, a concert, and even a few Chinese movies without subtitles, if you can believe it. So they decided to throw a party."

Burke and Gillian had to thread their way through a clump of white-coated teenagers to get to the lounge. The young hotel employees were watching the Westerners dance with fervent interest. Some of them were moving to the disco beat themselves. They clapped their hands over their heads, swung their hips, and sang along with the four-year-old disco tune.

"They'll be having their own party out here soon," Burke said. "Maybe we should invite them in."

"Don't, Burke. The management would raise a fuss." The rather small room was decorated with strings of

Christmas-tree lights hung from the ceiling. A record player was going full blast, playing the few records, which someone had picked up in Hong Kong, over and over again. Open bottles of liquor made wet circles on one table, and plates of hors d'oeuvres from the hotel kitchen sat on another.

Trent Baylor came forward to greet Burke and Gillian. "I'm glad you could make it."

"It looks like a good party," Burke said, surveying the crowded room. "Just about everyone came."

"A few of the guys still haven't showed." Trent laughed. "It's just as well. There are about ten times as many men as women. Maybe I'd better ask for a dance right now. Go get yourself a drink, Burke. I've got designs on your girl."

"Oh, no, you don't. You're too young to know this, but the first and the last dance belong to the guy the girl comes with."

The next number was a slow one. Burke took Gillian in his arms and moved off onto the small square in the middle of the floor kept clear for dancers. He held her close because of the crowd, but Gillian knew he would have even if they had been the only ones on the floor.

She stiffened against his encircling arm, trying to draw away from his body, pressing its length against hers, but he wouldn't permit it. He pulled her to him masterfully and kept her close as he skillfully led her around the small floor.

They passed Andrea, dancing stony-faced with the actor who played the husband she despised; and Robyn and Phil, cheek-to-cheek. Dan was in a corner with the makeup girl, his latest conquest.

When the music ended, Gillian felt shaken to the core. She thought she had been through too much with Burke ever to react to him again. But the slow dance, the feel of his broad shoulder under her hand, the touch of his hand on her waist, and the nearness of his body as they moved in unison were enough to stir up her senses. She didn't want his lips against her perfumed hair alone; she wanted them on her skin and mouth. She didn't want love words whispered into her ear; she wanted their warm breath against her lips. And no dance was as thrilling as the dance of love.

They danced together all evening. Burke never left Gillian's side, and when they danced no one cut in on him. For all his democratic ways, there was a magic circle around the famous director, a line people didn't lightly step over.

Gillian could sense Andrea's eyes on her, and from time to time she caught her staring with implacable hatred as Gillian danced with Burke, or accepted a drink from him, or stood by his side as he talked with somebody else at the party.

After a while the actress drifted over to Dan, and the makeup girl immediately walked away. Andrea sat down close to him and, laying her hand familiarly on his knee, became involved in animated conversation.

Gillian was sure the star was putting on an act, as always, this time in order to show that she too had a man—or perhaps it was even to make Burke jealous. But the effect of the older woman fawning on the young man was unpleasant. It was also drawing attention to her. People would look, then turn away, obviously to comment on what they had seen.

Burke kept glancing Andrea's way too, and his expression became increasingly gloomy. Finally he bent down and kissed Gillian quickly on the cheek.

"Excuse me a minute, darling, will you? I've got some company business to take care of."

She watched while his long legs carried him across the room. He nodded to Dan, then took Andrea's hands in his and talked earnestly to her. Andrea laughed artificially several times; then, still smiling as though something were a tremendous joke, she let Burke pull her to her feet. He put his arm around her shoulders, and together they left the room. Dan got up and rejoined the makeup girl.

The whole scene had been played out so quietly and naturally that only a few glances followed the couple as they left. And the curious quickly returned to their own pursuits.

Only Gillian stood, with blind eyes, staring at the doorway. At some point as she was watching Burke and Andrea, she had had a tremendous flash of insight. A man didn't treat a woman he loved as Burke treated Andrea. Burke never had behaved toward his star like a man in love. He was protective of her, but there was a world of difference between passion and protectiveness. Why he had this attitude toward the actress, Gillian did not know. She only knew that her heart was suffused with joy at her discovery.

And when he came back and took her in his arms for another slow dance, she melted into them instead of holding back. This time he lifted her thick, lustrous hair and kissed her pearly ear. But first he whispered, "I love you, Gillian. Truly, more than you can ever know."

It seemed to her that she took his words and held them to her heart, literally, as if they were a valentine. Everything in her life seemed to have taken on an intense rightness. She no longer cared about Andrea, but she was curious about what had just occurred.

"Dan isn't *that* much younger than Andrea," Burke began in answer to her question. "Even so, I didn't think it looked good for her to be flirting with him, when that rumor about her 'entertaining' young boys was going around."

He looked down at her, a mischievous glint in his eyes.

"Did you worry about my being in her room so long?"

Gillian shook her head and smiled. "Not this time. But . . ."

"Yes?"

"How did you get her to go to her room?"

"I told her she looked tired and maybe even a little haggard."

Gillian gave him a sidelong glance. "That was cruel. Remember when I called you an evil magician?"

"You bet I do." He paused. "I also remember what followed." He held his arm out to her. "Shall we?"

Gillian hesitated, her face beginning to flush with embarrassment. She looked around her. "What will everyone think?"

"Probably what the room boy thinks, and all the taxi drivers in Peking, and Keng, and the entire cast and crew of *Siege,* namely, that I am absolutely crazy-nuts about you, that I can't look at anyone but you, can't stand not being with you, and can't keep my hands off of you. C'mon."

As it turned out, no one even noticed them leaving for by this time the party was in full swing. The small, crowded lounge was thick with cigarette smoke, the music had reached a level hitherto unheard-of in China, people were indiscriminately shouting intimacies and trivialities at one another, and the hall outside the lounge was filled with room boys, laundry girls, and desk clerks discoing with swivel-hipped wild abandon.

"This is one night we don't have to worry about the room boy," Burke said. He looked down at Gillian with an exciting mixture of amusement, desire, and love as he pressed the up button in the elevator.

Walking down the hall with him beside her, Gillian was aquiver with the desire their close dancing had aroused. But once they were in her room, a last vestige of resistance asserted itself. Burke had caused her so much heartbreak, she couldn't help but want to punish him a little.

Facing him, she could feel the hot flush of anger at past wrongs mount in her cheeks. She threw her head back in a gesture that said, "look out," and her heavy brown hair swung from side to side.

He watched her through narrowed, bright-blue eyes.

"I like you that way." His voice was husky, his eyes passion-fired. His intense face was that of a man who took what he wanted.

In one step, he had taken her in his arms with a tender violence. The feel of his hands on her slender form made her forget everything but the joy of the moment. She put her hands on his cheeks, relishing the feel of his rough male skin, and pulled his face down to hers. Closing her eyes, she examined it with her fingers, tracing his straight brows, the plane of his cheeks down to that stubborn jaw, the bridge of his aquiline nose. '

Would she ever know him, she wondered, as she knew his face? He was like a diamond with hundreds of facets. Each one revealed a different Burke Ferrara, but underneath there was only one man, a single, whole personality, the man she loved.

"Don't ever leave me, Gillian," he whispered into the soft masses of her perfumed hair. "I don't give a damn about the rest of the world. No one out there can hurt me . . . only you can."

His mouth seized hers in an explosion of love. Ardently they covered each other's mouth and face with quick, hungry kisses. He pulled her against him, his hands curving lightly, firmly around her hips. She exulted in the soft curves of her body as they met his male hardness. She reached up to him and brushed her lips against his. She would have done it again, but he didn't give her the chance.

His lips covered hers in a scorching kiss that aroused her to fever pitch. As he imprinted tiny love bites at the corners of her mouth, his hands caressed her, smoothing themselves against the upward swell of her breasts, shaping themselves to her hips, lightly stroking her thighs.

He undid the lacings on one shoulder and slipped her dress down. He left a trail of slow-burning kisses along her slim white shoulder then gently, carefully, as though her body were infinitely precious to him, he lifted her silken shoulder strap and kissed her tenderly there.

Releasing her bra, he trailed his lips down to where her breast rose, snowy, with a pink center. He kissed the soft flesh, then caressed the upward-straining tip with his tongue, sending tremors of delight through her.

He ran his hands roughly over her body then, so that she shuddered under his touch—a long, gasping quiver that ran the length of her and made Burke draw his breath in sharply.

"Love me tonight, Gillian, as, so help me, I love you."

He undid the other shoulder lacings and slipped her dress off. And when she finally stood proud and full-bodied before him, the moonlight silvering her skin, she slipped her hands under his shirt and down the rough surface of his jeans till he too was moonlit and ready.

The night was tender, filled with words and acts of love. Gillian's heavy hair fell around them like a dark waterfall. She was a mermaid in love with a mortal . . . an enchantress. They were lovers drowning in each other, going deeper and deeper together into a world of awesome beauty and joy. And when the moon set, they were still murmuring, "I love you" against each other's lips.

chapter 11

GILLIAN WOKE UP the next morning in a delirium of happiness. She felt an overwhelming need to celebrate, and put on a dress she hadn't worn before—a cotton print in peach and pale apple-green with a ruffled collar and cuffs.

She stood at the window, a cup of instant coffee in her hand, and watched the hotel employees go through the slow, postured movements of *t'ai chi ch'uan* in the park, by the fish pond. There were one hundred twenty-eight movements to this form of calisthenics, which took about fifteen minutes to execute. The name meant "ultimate supreme boxing." Originally it had been a weaponless combat discipline, but had developed into a combination of shadow boxing and ballet.

Gillian's attention soon wandered from the graceful poised motions, and she looked off into the distance, recalling her night of love with Burke. It seemed to her that the love affair each of them had with life itself—

their love of purposeful work, accomplishment, companionship, and fun—had overflowed in a torrent of joy and excitement. She felt that in loving each other, they had reaffirmed their love for themselves and for life.

That was what Elliot had lacked—joy in being. Therefore he couldn't be a source of joy to anyone else.

She set her cup down and, looking at herself in the streaked wardrobe mirror, smiled at the blurred image. It had the soft, ripe, gentle look of a woman fulfilled.

When there was a rap at her door, she knew instinctively that it was Burke. He smiled at her in a special, loving way and said softly, "Good morning, China Girl. Ready?"

They walked down the long hall, pausing to say good morning to the room boy. When they turned the corner and Gillian took a step in front of him, Burke stopped her, sweeping his arm around her waist. Holding her tight, he lifted her thick hair off her neck and trailed his lips across the bare skin, giving a final, exciting nibble to the lobe of her right ear.

He turned her around then and looked down into her face. "I had to say good morning the right way, the only way I'll be doing it from now on."

"I think you just like to kiss me in provocative places."

"The more provocative, the better," he answered blandly.

Gillian heard a step coming down the hall. "It's the room boy!"

Burke rolled his eyes. "Wanting to see how it's done, no doubt."

When they reached the lobby, where the usual crowd was waiting for the bus, Gillian noticed Robyn wasn't there. It seemed unlikely that she would have left early with the stars, because then she would have been in Andrea's company, a situation Robyn avoided if she could.

Gillian didn't want to draw Burke's attention to Robyn's absence just when he was becoming somewhat more understanding of the actress. She eyed the desk clerk's phone, thinking she would call Robyn's room, but Burke didn't leave her side. Thrilling as this was, it meant that all she could do was watch the stairs, hoping against hope that Robyn would appear. Finally Gillian told Burke she had forgotten something and would have to go to her room for it.

"The bus'll be here in a minute," he warned her.

"I won't be long. I promise."

He gave her a sharp look. He knows I'm not telling the truth, she thought. But the truth might mean compromising Robyn. Burke would be sure to think she had a hangover, which was Gillian's secret fear too.

Gillian ran up the stairs and went directly to Robyn's room. She knocked once, and when there was no answer, opened the door and went in. The curtains were closed. Robyn was just a mound of white bedclothes in the dark room.

Quickly Gillian opened the curtains and raised the window sash, flooding the room with sunshine and fresh air. Stirring a little, Robyn muttered, "Somebody turn out the light."

"It's morning, Robyn," Gillian said testily. "Everyone's downstairs waiting for the bus. Hurry and get up. You can take a taxi to the set. The desk boy will get one for you."

"I can't, Gillie. I'm *so* tired! And I think I have a cold coming on, too. No kidding. I'm played out."

"Force yourself. Do you still have some instant coffee? I'll make you a cup. Then I've got to go."

"On the table by that green seaweed they call tea."

Gillian poured hot water over a spoonful of powdered coffee and handed the cup to Robyn.

"Here, drink this. Then make yourself get up and get dressed. I'm leaving right this minute. Burke will be mad if I hold up the bus."

She stared down at Robyn, noting her white face and puffy eyes.

"I don't have a hangover, if that's what you're thinking. I'm through with that whole drinking scene. Phil and I are getting married."

"Robyn, how wonderful! Phil's a marvelous guy."

"You're telling me!" Robyn looked at her slyly. "Maybe we'll make it a double one, huh? You and Burke, me and Phil."

Gillian just smiled and started for the door.

"Gillie?"

She stopped and turned. Robyn was sitting on the side of the bed now, her feet on the floor.

"Can you come back this afternoon or tonight after work? There's something I want to tell you."

Gillian gestured impatiently. She had to hurry. "Sure, Robyn."

"It's something I think you should know. Something about Burke and that female viper he was married to, the great star Andrea Steele."

Gillian stopped short, one hand on the doorknob. Intuitively she knew Robyn's story was the one she had been waiting to hear.

"I'll come back. See you on the set . . ." And she left the room. This time she took the stairs slowly, turning over in her mind all the things Robyn might tell her. She was afraid of what she would hear, but Gillian also knew she would go back to Robyn's room. She had to.

When she reached the lobby, she found it empty except for Burke, pacing up and down with long, impatient strides.

"Where the hell have you been? I called your room, and there was no answer. I've got a bus full of people out there waiting for you. If it were anybody else, I'd fire 'em on the spot."

With a sidelong smile, Gillian went up to him and placed a finger gently on his lips.

"Robyn wasn't feeling well. I went to her room to get her going. She's taking a taxi."

Burke kissed her finger, then took it in his mouth and gave it a tiny but sharp bite.

"Women!"

"Yes?" She looked at him sternly, questioning him with raised eyebrows.

"They're wonderful," he said good-naturedly.

"You don't mean it," she purred.

"You're damn right I don't. C'mon, let's get going. I've got a film to bring in."

The film company's luck had turned. Robyn showed up in time to be made up and costumed for her scene. Andrea assumed her glacial-goddess pose again, keeping herself aloof from everyone on the set but responding to Burke's direction with complete professionalism. Nobody blew any lines. No equipment was missing. And Gillian didn't find anything to take exception to. They even finished early in the afternoon.

When she got to her room, Gillian took a long, relaxing shower and put on the green silk kimono she had bought in the Peking Department Store. She lay down on the satin spread for a nap, but the sight of the dragons going in opposite directions was overwhelming.

She got up to take off the spread, then changed her mind about sleeping. The story Robyn promised her had been on her mind all day. Surely she was in her room by now.

Gillian dressed quickly, throwing the robe on the bed.

Robyn answered with a slightly slurred, "Yes?" when Gillian knocked.

"It's Gillian."

"Just a sec."

Gillian could have laughed. Robyn was wearing her dragon kimono, a twin to the one Gillian had just taken off. It seemed a long time ago that she had first seen Robyn wearing it in the lobby when she complained about a mouse in her room.

"I was asleep, Gillie, but that's all right. I'm glad to see you."

"I was going to take a nap myself. I guess we're all tired."

"At least we'll be going home soon. A few more scenes, and then it's goodbye Peking, hello Hollywood. And let me tell you, I'm ready. How about some tea or coffee?"

"No, thanks. You were going to tell me something . . ."

"Yeah. Of course, you have to remember that I only heard this story secondhand. It happened long before my time." Robyn St. Regis's acknowledged age was as fictional as the films she appeared in.

"Of course," Gillian said politely.

"Do you know why Burke's so good to her, Gillie?"

"No, why?"

Robyn paused dramatically. "Guilt!"

Gillian's heart sank. What had Burke done? Fearfully she asked, "Guilt about what?"

"The accident. On the way to Palm Springs. You heard about it, didn't you?"

Gillian nodded. This must be the accident to which Paul Rogers had referred.

"Burke was driving. And Andrea was hurt—badly. So badly that when she finally got out of the hospital, she had to hole up on a ranch in Oregon for a long time, waiting for the scars to heal before she could go back to work. And naturally, being Andrea, she laid a heavy guilt trip on Burke."

"Did you ever hear any stories about Andrea's . . . er . . . 'entertaining' young boys at that ranch?"

Robyn looked delighted. "No, did she?"

"I don't think so," Gillian said hurriedly. "It's just a nasty rumor."

Robyn stared gloomily at the floor. "I wouldn't put it past her."

Gillian's heart began beating fast. She wasn't sure she

wanted to ask the question that was on her mind. It made her feel unpleasant even to think about it, because it showed a lack of trust in Burke. But she had to know.

"Were Burke and Andrea lovers after the divorce?"

"No. I saw a lot of them in those days, so I would have known," Robyn replied, tacitly acknowledging that she had fibbed about the event's occurring "long before my time." "We went to the same parties. A man like Burke doesn't have trouble getting women, and Andrea didn't exactly go into a nunnery after the divorce. That story about her and young boys is just garbage. She's got the morals of a rattlesnake, but she'd never have to resort to that."

A tremendous surge of relief and happiness swept over Gillian. Burke hadn't lied to her. It was Hank Simpson to whom he had lied when he said he and Andrea had been lovers.

She got up and said feelingly, "Thanks, Robyn. Thanks a lot. I have one more question, though."

"Sure thing. Shoot."

"Why didn't you tell me this before?"

"I didn't tell you before because it's ancient history and the studio doesn't like people digging up old dirt. Also"—Robyn hesitated—"I don't like Andrea. I never have and I never will. But I think I understand her. She's like a lot of actors and actresses I've known." Robyn looked at Gillian intently as though to make sure she understood. "You see, Gillie, there's nothing there. I mean, when Andrea isn't performing, she's nobody. She doesn't have a personality of her own. Maybe that's why she's such a good actress. I don't know. But anyway, I wouldn't be too hard on her if I were you."

Gillian nodded thoughtfully. What Robyn had just told her fit her impression of Andrea. She seemed to come alive only when she was before the cameras, when she was given a ready-made identity to slip into. This was something Burke must have known, and that, given the marvelous richness of his personality, would have made

Andrea as unsuited to him as Elliot had been to Gillian.

"I understand completely," she said. "But why did you decide to tell me about the accident now?"

"Because I thought you might be getting some wrong signals about why Burke looks out for her all the time."

"I was getting wrong signals for a while, but I'm not any more." Gillian's voice sang. She gave Robyn a quick hug and left.

When she got back to her room, Gillian undressed quickly and, with the green kimono tied loosely about her, lay down on the bed. She heard water running and listened awhile, puzzled. Then she got up to investigate.

The hotel bathrooms lacked shower curtains, so the first thing she saw was a tanned, muscular back covered with cascading soapsuds. She gasped, and Burke turned his head, a wide grin on his face.

Genuinely shocked, Gillian cried out, "What are you doing here?"

"It's called taking a shower. Mine didn't work, so the management said I could use yours."

"Baloney! How about the room boy?" she wailed.

"He's no problem. I told him I wouldn't steal your towels. Where've you been? I've been waiting for you to get back and . . . er, shall we say, fill that kimono."

Gillian looked at him reproachfully, a look he ignored as he ran his eyes over the areas of flesh exposed by the loosened robe. He had turned completely and was facing her now. Legs spread, hands on lean hips, he was a figure of primeval virility. Pouting a little, Gillian closed her robe around her. She wasn't about to play nymph to his pagan god.

She gave him a second, disapproving look.

His vivid blue eyes narrowed in amusement. "Is something wrong? We're going formal, perhaps?" Then, coaxingly, "Come on in, the water's fine."

"No, Burke, you come out."

In answer, he reached out a long arm and gave her robe a tweak that pulled it halfway off her. Then he stood looking at her, a challenge in his eyes.

"Scared?"

With a haughty lift of her slim, golden-brown eyebrows, she stepped out of the robe and into the rusty tub. She sniffed at his fresh, soap-and-water smell. His long-ish hair was dripping. Water glistened on the springy virile hair on his chest. She longed to bury her hand in its thick wet mat, but she didn't. She was really put out with him.

He didn't touch her. Looking down at her, he said, "It might interest you to know, my Puritan petal, that I slipped in my own prewar bathtub and almost knocked myself unconscious. See? I've got a bump right here." He pointed to a slight swelling on his forehead.

Smiling to herself, she admitted defeat. She gave him a sidelong glance of disbelief and said dryly, "I'll kiss it and make it well." She pulled his head down to her and put her lips to the bump.

"I've got another one here."

Gillian took his finger away from his right cheek and kissed him there too.

"And there's a really bad one on my finger. Somebody weaker would have required stitches." He held his finger out to her.

A sardonic gleam came into Gillian's eye. "It looks all right to me."

Burke examined his finger closely. "You're right. It's all cured. I have terrific healing powers, inherited from my forebears, who were too cheap to go to a doctor. It's carried in the genes. Just think how much money we'll save on Band-Aids for the kids."

He put his hands on her shoulders. "Is there anything *you* want kissed and made well?"

"Just me," she said softly.

He rained watery kisses on her face. Then he lifted

her wet hair and trailed his lips across her throat and the nape of her neck, feathering her skin all the while with light finger touches.

A delicious anticipation seized her. She threw her head back and laughed exultantly. She felt like some wild thing coming to a man whose hands knew what to do with her.

"Let me wash you." He spoke tenderly, and his hands were gentle as he passed the bar of pink, geranium-scented soap over her firm breasts and rounded hips. Her wet skin felt slick under his touch. The sensation was new and infinitely exciting.

She ran her hands slowly all the way down his back. "You've got sexy skin. Did you know that?"

"Of course," he said haughtily. "I won an award for it one year—'The Director with the Sexiest Skin.'"

"What would I win an award for?" She giggled and wound her arms around his neck. "Tell me."

"All rumors notwithstanding, Hollywood does *not* give an award for what you're good at. Mink coats maybe, jobs, stardom. But not a public award."

Playfully she put her hands against his chest and gave him a little shove. He caught her in his arms then and tried to kiss all her freckles, while she giggled again, this time at the thought of what Elliot would say if he saw her in such an unconventional place. Burke had just found a freckle Gillian knew didn't exist, on the upward swell of her rosy-tipped breast, when she screamed. The water had turned icy!

"I think we've used all their hot water," Burke said with a laugh. He turned the old-fashioned knobs and reached for the towels hanging on a rod. Quickly he put one around himself, then used the other to pat Gillian dry. She let herself flow into his hands, gave herself over to them, thrilled to the feel of them on her flesh under the soft terry cloth.

His hands cupping her breasts, he brought his mouth down and brushed his lips across hers in great sweeps of passion. Then he plunged his tongue into the warm tenderness of her mouth, ending with gentle love bites at the corners of her mouth.

He dropped the towel to her waist and lowered his lips to the soft flesh of her breast. Slowly he followed the tracery of blue veins under the milky white skin. And when the rosy center of each breast was firm with arousal, he took each pebble-hard nipple in his mouth and lightly tugged at it.

Wild with excitement, Gillian felt everything within her opening up to him. The smoky male smell of him, his demanding, aggressive mouth, his hard, virile body were her universe—the only one she wanted. With a slight movement, she let the towel fall from her. She wanted no encumbrance to their love. Then suddenly, masterfully, he was lifting her off the floor and carrying her in his strong arms to the bed.

He laid her tenderly down and covered her body with his. His murmured, "I love you, Gillian," was the prelude to a performance he directed with consummate artistry as he slowly took her from one level of excitement to the next, till the final crescendo swept her away in a burst of star fire.

Sated and exquisitely satisfied, Gillian lay in his arms, watching the sunshine dapple their bodies with lacy patterns as the curtains moved in the light breeze. Idly she passed her finger through these splashes of gold on his skin while she listened to the bicycle bells softly peal their song again.

"When did you know?" she asked musingly, drawing a circle with one finger around his nipples. If she enjoyed that, why wouldn't he?

"That I loved you?" He laughed, his blue eyes sharp with amusement. "The first time we met, when you stood there in your historical-consultant's uniform and gave me hell about the scene with the Western ladies walking the street. You were absolutely adorable."

She tweaked one of the hairs on his chest. "It wasn't a historical-consultant's uniform! It was a very attractive business suit."

"Not nearly so attractive as what you don't have on now," he said seductively, sliding his hands around her.

She let him pull her in even closer to him, but arched her back so she could look up into his face. "And I thought, when we met, that you were arrogant, unreasonable, and bad-tempered."

After he had kissed her in a spot she wouldn't have allowed anyone to touch just a few days ago, he said, "That's because I was scared silly that you might not love me. And with good reason, when you kept freezing up on me."

She drew her finger across the hard muscles of his abdomen where the line of tan ended, and felt him quiver. "I was afraid too. I couldn't afford to be hurt so soon after Elliot, especially when I saw how close you were to Andrea."

Suddenly Burke was solemn. "I haven't loved Andrea for a long, long time."

"I know that now, Burke. But it would have helped if you had told me about the accident you and Andrea were in. Why didn't you?"

She felt his stomach go rigid under her fingertips.

"Told you *what* about the accident?" he asked sharply.

"That you were driving and Andrea was badly injured. Robyn told me."

He was silent for a long time. Gillian lay perfectly still beside him. She wondered if he was angry with her for repeating the gossip.

"Andrea wasn't injured in that accident," he said finally. "It was hardly an accident at all. The studio just used it as a pretext for her to go into seclusion."

"Why did she have to go into seclusion, Burke?" Gillian's voice was low and gentle.

"She was on drugs—she was a heavy user. That ranch in Oregon was afterward, after she had been in a sanitarium and when she still wasn't ready to return to Hollywood."

Gillian was stunned. The thought of that beautiful, talented woman a slave to a pernicious habit was horrifying. In spite of Andrea's malice toward her, Gillian was swept by a wave of sympathy for the actress.

A moment later she realized that Robyn's explanation of why Burke was so protective of Andrea wasn't true. Gillian decided to take the plunge and force everything out into the open. She and Burke could never have a trusting relationship if the ghost of Andrea hovered over them.

"Robyn thought the accident accounted for your feelings of guilt."

"Guilt? How would Robyn know how I felt?" His muscles tightened again. She smoothed her hand over his stomach to relax them. "My guilt, such as it was, or as I saw it," he continued dryly, "lay in having driven Andrea too hard. We continued to work together after the divorce. I was the director who made her a star. Every single one of our pictures was a success. But I didn't take her vulnerability into account. I knew she was terribly immature, of course—I had been married to her for two years. But she was ambitious as hell, too. I thought she could take the constant work and pressure involved in the perfection I demand—from myself as well as others. But she couldn't. She considered herself a failure—although, believe me, she wasn't—and resorted to drugs to escape and to feel good. And you know how that goes. Her use just kept escalating, till she had to be treated.

"Once I knew all this, I felt guilty as the devil, and rightly so. I hadn't used my imagination, I hadn't *bothered,* to figure out what was going on inside her. I don't know, maybe there was even some subconscious resentment left over from our marriage that made me less understanding than I should have been. At any rate, as soon as I knew she was hooked on drugs, I started taking care of her. I was determined to get her back on her feet and acting again. I found a good sanitarium for her and insisted that the studio protect her reputation while she was there. I also insisted that she not be rushed back into acting before she was ready, and bought that ranch for her, so she could convalesce," Burke explained, and Gillian knew each word rekindled unpleasant memories. "When she really was all right, I insisted that she be given the lead in *Siege,* which I had already been asked to direct. She's doing a terrific job. The film will be a success; I'm sure of it. I'm also certain it'll put Andrea right back there at the top, where she belongs. But there's only so much one person can do for another. And frankly I think I've done it. The slate is clean."

Gillian was moved by his explanation and overwhelmingly relieved to finally know the truth.

"But why didn't you tell me this earlier?" she asked. "I would have understood."

"It involved someone else's privacy. Andrea doesn't want anyone to know about that episode in her life."

"I understand," Gillian said quietly. Her own acute sense of privacy made Burke's explanation entirely reasonable to her.

"And if at times I seemed overly solicitous of Andrea," he continued, "don't forget that I had an obligation to the studio as well as to her. Remember I told you once Andrea was an emotional waif? Well, I had to keep that waif working, for both her own and the studio's sake. That meant keeping her on a fairly even keel day after day."

"Does she still love you, do you think?"

Burke laughed. "Not really. Andrea's a collector. She doesn't like to see a piece get away from her."

His laugh released them both from the trauma of the past. They made love again, wordlessly, thrillingly. They had passed beyond the stage of primal urgency now, and could take the time to arouse each other slowly, to discover what the other really wanted, and to satisfy that desire with imaginative ardor.

Afterward, exhausted and happy, they fell asleep cuddled together. Much later Gillian awoke, with Burke's arm across her breast and his thigh pressed against hers. With that sensitivity they had to each other, he awakened too.

He folded her in his arms. "I'm going to be wrapping up the film very soon now—the part to be shot in China, anyway. I've heard about a Swedish yacht I can charter. It's sailing out of Shanghai, up the Yangtze. It's just what I've always wanted—to get you on a slow boat in China. We can be married by the U. S. consul."

"I haven't said 'yes' yet. Don't I get a choice?"

"Actually, no, you don't." He brought his lips down on hers then and rekindled the bright flame that was always there waiting for him.

"Where would we live, Burke? My work's in Haywood and yours is in Hollywood."

"That's no problem. I'm going to be directing a play in New York in the fall. Haywood's not far. After that, don't worry, we'll find a way to be together."

She lay in his arms while his hands gently caressed her, and dreamed of their honeymoon ship rocking on the water, and of a narrow berth just big enough for a man and woman to become one, the *yang* and *yin* that together created "all that comes to be."

As he reached down to kiss her, she murmured, "Keng is going to miss us."

"We'll send him pictures of the kids."

When his warm lips reached hers, she returned his kiss passionately, knowing she had found all the love and excitement and sensuality she would ever need.

Second Chance at Love

_____ 06195-6 SHAMROCK SEASON #35 Jennifer Rose
_____ 06304-5 HOLD FAST TIL MORNING #36 Beth Brookes
_____ 06282-0 HEARTLAND #37 Lynn Fairfax
_____ 06408-4 FROM THIS DAY FORWARD #38 Jolene Adams
_____ 05968-4 THE WIDOW OF BATH #39 Anne Devon
_____ 06400-9 CACTUS ROSE #40 Zandra Colt
_____ 06401-7 PRIMITIVE SPLENDOR #41 Katherine Swinford
_____ 06424-6 GARDEN OF SILVERY DELIGHTS #42 Sharon Francis
_____ 06521-8 STRANGE POSSESSION #43 Johanna Phillips
_____ 06326-6 CRESCENDO #44 Melinda Harris
_____ 05818-1 INTRIGUING LADY #45 Daphne Woodward
_____ 06547-1 RUNAWAY LOVE #46 Jasmine Craig
_____ 06423-8 BITTERSWEET REVENGE #47 Kelly Adams
_____ 06541-2 STARBURST #48 Tess Ewing
_____ 06540-4 FROM THE TORRID PAST #49 Ann Cristy
_____ 06544-7 RECKLESS LONGING #50 Daisy Logan
_____ 05851-3 LOVE'S MASQUERADE #51 Lillian Marsh
_____ 06148-4 THE STEELE HEART #52 Jocelyn Day
_____ 06422-X UNTAMED DESIRE #53 Beth Brookes
_____ 06651-6 VENUS RISING #54 Michelle Roland
_____ 06595-1 SWEET VICTORY #55 Jena Hunt
_____ 06575-7 TOO NEAR THE SUN #56 Aimée Duvall
_____ 05625-1 MOURNING BRIDE #57 Lucia Curzon
_____ 06411-4 THE GOLDEN TOUCH #58 Robin James
_____ 06596-X EMBRACED BY DESTINY #59 Simone Hadary
_____ 06660-5 TORN ASUNDER #60 Ann Cristy
_____ 06573-0 MIRAGE #61 Margie Michaels
_____ 06650-8 ON WINGS OF MAGIC #62 Susanna Collins

All of the above titles are $1.75 per copy

Available at your local bookstore or return this form to:

SECOND CHANCE AT LOVE
Book Mailing Service
P.O. Box 690, Rockville Cntr., NY 11570

Please enclose 75¢ for postage and handling for one book, 25¢ each
add'l. book ($1.50 max.). No cash, CODs or stamps. Total amount
enclosed: $ _____ in check or money order.

NAME _____

ADDRESS _____

CITY _____ STATE/ZIP_____

Allow six weeks for delivery   SK-41

_____ 05816-5 **DOUBLE DECEPTION #63** Amanda Troy
_____ 06675-3 **APOLLO'S DREAM #64** Claire Evans
_____ 06676-1 **SMOLDERING EMBERS #65** Marie Charles
_____ 06677-X **STORMY PASSAGE #66** Laurel Blake
_____ 06678-8 **HALFWAY THERE #67** Aimée Duvall
_____ 06679-6 **SURPRISE ENDING #68** Elinor Stanton
_____ 06680-X **THE ROGUE'S LADY #69** Anne Devon
_____ 06681-8 **A FLAME TOO FIERCE #70** Jan Mathews
_____ 06682-6 **SATIN AND STEELE #71** Jaelyn Conlee
_____ 06683-4 **MIXED DOUBLES #72** Meredith Kingston
_____ 06684-2 **RETURN ENGAGEMENT #73** Kay Robbins
_____ 06685-0 **SULTRY NIGHTS #74** Ariel Tierney
_____ 06686-9 **AN IMPROPER BETROTHMENT #75** Henrietta Houston
_____ 06687-7 **FORSAKING ALL OTHERS #76** LaVyrle Spencer
_____ 06688-5 **BEYOND PRIDE #77** Kathleen Ash
_____ 06689-3 **SWEETER THAN WINE #78** Jena Hunt
_____ 06690-7 **SAVAGE EDEN #79** Diane Crawford
_____ 06691-5 **STORMY REUNION #80** Jasmine Craig
_____ 06692-3 **THE WAYWARD WIDOW #81** Anne Mayfield
_____ 06693-1 **TARNISHED RAINBOW #82** Jocelyn Day
_____ 06694-X **STARLIT SEDUCTION #83** Anne Reed
_____ 06695-8 **LOVER IN BLUE #84** Aimée Duvall
_____ 06696-6 **THE FAMILIAR TOUCH #85** Lynn Lawrence
_____ 06697-4 **TWILIGHT EMBRACE #86** Jennifer Rose
_____ 06698-2 **QUEEN OF HEARTS #87** Lucia Curzon
_____ 06850-0 **PASSION'S SONG #88** Johanna Phillips
_____ 06851-9 **A MAN'S PERSUASION #89** Katherine Granger
_____ 06852-7 **FORBIDDEN RAPTURE #90** Kate Nevins
_____ 06853-5 **THIS WILD HEART #91** Margarett McKean
_____ 06854-3 **SPLENDID SAVAGE #92** Zandra Colt
_____ 06855-1 **THE EARL'S FANCY #93** Charlotte Hines

All of the above titles are $1.75 per copy

Available at your local bookstore or return this form to:

SECOND CHANCE AT LOVE
Book Mailing Service
P.O. Box 690, Rockville Cntr., NY 11570

Please enclose 75¢ for postage and handling for one book, 25¢ each add'l. book ($1.50 max.). No cash, CODs or stamps. Total amount enclosed: $ _____ in check or money order.

NAME _____

ADDRESS _____

CITY _____ STATE/ZIP _____

Allow six weeks for delivery.   SK-41

WHAT READERS SAY ABOUT
SECOND CHANCE AT LOVE BOOKS

"Your books are the greatest!"
    —*M. N., Carteret, New Jersey**

"I have been reading romance novels for quite some time, but the SECOND CHANCE AT LOVE books are the most enjoyable."
    —*P. R., Vicksburg, Mississippi**

"I enjoy SECOND CHANCE [AT LOVE] more than any books that I have read and I do read a lot."
    —*J. R., Gretna, Louisiana**

"For years I've had my subscription in to Harlequin. Currently there is a series called Circle of Love, but you have them all beat."
    —*C. B., Chicago, Illinois**

"I really think your books are exceptional...I read Harlequin and Silhouette and although I still like them, I'll buy your books over theirs. SECOND CHANCE [AT LOVE] is more interesting and holds your attention and imagination with a better story line..."
    —*J. W., Flagstaff, Arizona**

"I've read many romances, but yours take the 'cake'!"
    —*D. H., Bloomsburg, Pennsylvania**

"Have waited ten years for *good* romance books. Now I have them."
    —*M. P., Jacksonville, Florida**

*Names and addresses available upon request